LYNTON
AND
THE CAPE TOWN GHOST

By

J. Wayne Frye

#13 in the Lynton Series

An Old Tale of Mystery
With a Modern Twist

Lynton and the Cape Town Ghost

TO:

Joe Coddington – Oh, what a wonderful friendship we had as young adults in Sicklerville, New Jersey. Those were days when all things were possible and no mountain was too high to climb. How we threw caution to the wind!

Also, as always, to my muse:
Lynton Globa Viñas – the dynamic dynamo.

Catalogue Number: 971389-2018

ISBN: 978-1-928183-38-9

Fireside Books – Canadian Division
Part of the Peninsula Publishing Consortium

Lynton and the Cape Town Ghost

Table of Contents

Lynton and the Cape Town Ghost

About the Author

Wayne Frye's *Aaron Adams* mysteries, *Chablis Louise Chavez* thrillers, *Girl* books and *Lynton* adventures titillate the brains of those who enjoy tantalizing tales of mystery. Growing up in the small town of Asheboro, North Carolina, he wrote his first novel at 15, but waited over twenty years before finally sending it to a publisher. His life, like the heroes he writes about, has been filled with adventure and excitement. He has been a college hockey coach, professor, and at one time, the youngest university president in the USA. Called a marketing genius by the *Los Angeles Times*, he has been a promotional consultant to hockey teams and motion picture companies. He has been cited for his work with inner-city gangs in Los Angeles and is active in the anti-globalization movement. A proud Canadian, he divides his time between Ladysmith, British Columbia and Cape Town, South Africa.

Some of the 46 books by J. Wayne Frye

Hockey Mania and the Mystery of Nancy Running Elk
Something Evil in the Darkness at Hopkins House
White Meteors and the Ghost of Sue Ann McGee
How Hockey Saved a Jew From the Holocaust
The Girl Who Said Goodbye for the Last Time
The Girl Who Motivated Murder Most Foul
The Girl Who Stirred up the Whirlwind
The Girl Who Rode into a Storm
Fall From Apocalypse
Armageddon Now
Sammy Sasquatch and the Sts'ailes Star
Worth Part 1: Roaring Through Life Like a Comet in the Midnight Sky
Worth Part 2: The Night of Thunder Road
When Jesus Came to Jersey as the Son of Thunder
When Jesus Came to Canada to Lead an Indigenous Rebellion
When Jesus Came to the Black Hills to do the Ghost Dance
Lynton Curls Her Hair
Lynton Walks on Water
Lynton and the Vampire at Tagaytay Manor
Lynton Buys a Cell-Phone and Hears the Voice of Doom
Lynton Viñas and Beowulf Perez in the Taal Inferno
Lynton and the Ghosts in the Mansion on Balete Drive
Lynton Viñas: Shadow in the Darkness
Lynton's South African Adventure
Lynton, the Karoo Vampire and the Jewels of Omar Bin Abi
Lynton and the Stellenbosch Terror
Chablis: Avenging Angel for the Forgotten
In the City of Lost Hope
Chablis and the Terrorist
Pursuit
The Disappearance
Points of Rebellion: Aboriginals Who Fought for Justice
Trumped in America

J. Wayne Frye

Prologue
Whirlpool of Swirling Wretchedness

Lynton Viñas is a woman who rarely seeks adventure, but somehow it always seems to find her no matter how remote a location she may be in, because some people are like magnets when it comes to excitement, especially when they see agony in the faces of others. They see suffering and ask why? They see misery and their hearts palpitate with empathy. Lynton Viñas, renowned demon fighter and sometimes able aide to famous private eye, Chablis Louise Chavez, always reaches out with the hand of compassion to those who suffer in a world where there is almost no empathy from those who are too self-absorbed and obsessed with wealth to care about others.

Lynton and the Cape Town Ghost

Ordinarily, people of wealth have few of the problems that burden the less economically fortunate. That is the way of a world where greed is the norm, rather than the exception. However, Lynton was the extreme exception. She knew the sting of being poor, but through tenaciousness she had clawed her way up from the pit of poverty-stricken despair that afflicts about 50% of the world, with another 30% just holding on by a slender thread that keeps them from falling into the abyss that waits to swallow those with meagre means. Despite her success, she never looked disparagingly upon those who toiled in obscurity for their daily bread. She saw nobleness in those who had to endure neglect from governments that were there to serve the privileged and corporations, rather than those who were ground up by the evil machinery of capitalism. Now, in the most unusual of places, she was gazing at a rich young girl, and in that face she saw an agony that tugged at her heart. Alas, those who look with compassion upon those suffering, often themselves, wind up in the middle of a turbulent sea where a whirlpool of intrigue and mystery awaits to pull the kind sojourner into darkness. Lynton was about to tumble head first into that whirlpool of swirling wretchedness.

Chapter 1
Embrace Her Daughter in its Malevolence

A young girl sat shivering in a corner of the luxurious penthouse living room at the swank Belvedere Grand Hotel overlooking the waterfront in Cape Town, South Africa. The penthouse was occupied by Ann Shriver, widely known all over the world as the woman behind the Shriver Cosmetics empire, and the shivering fourteen year old girl that was her only child, the reserved and observant, Alice Shriver.

Alice was quivering with anticipation as she looked out an open window that welcomed the summer breeze and the generous sunshine. Despite the open window, the air conditioning was pumping cold air into the room, but that was not the cause of the shivering she was experiencing. No, it was something far more foreboding.

To the right of the window, an attractive middle-aged woman in a long black dress sat reading. Alice took a deep breath and turned her gaze anxiously upon the doorway that led to the corridor, and spasmodic shudders swept through her body due to nervous fear.

The room was still, and despite the sun shinning in through the window, there was an intense darkness to the place, not physical darkness, but emotional darkness. When Alice's governess, Brandy Gorham, looked up from her book, as she turned the page, so quiet was the room that the mere rustle of the page seemed like a scream. Page after page was turned over a period of time, and Alice cringed with each turn of a page. It was as if the noise of the turning page was a dagger into her soul, as she kept looking intensely at the bedroom door.

It seemed ages before the outer door of the penthouse suite received a knock and the butler finally opened the door and into the vestibule entered a tall, thin, white-haired man who moved swiftly toward Alice. She quickly turned and came to him, her eyes, big and pleading, reading his face with dramatic intentness.

Smiling, he said, "Well, Alice, how nice to see you. Now, what is the urgency I see in your demeanour, my dear?"

"May I please see my mother now, Doctor Holcomb?" She asked.

He shook his head and almost whispered, "No."

"Please," she pleaded.

"Not just yet, Alice," he gently replied, and noting her deep breath of disappointment he added, "Why, I haven't seen her myself this morning. I need to check her first."

Again, with tears now in her eyes, she said, "Please."

The middle-aged physician looked down upon the girl. "Disturbing her now would not be a good idea. We must let her have peace, quiet and much rest."

"I won't disturb her. There's a nurse in there all the time. Why should I disturb my mother more than a nurse?" asked Alice.

He evaded the question and shrugged his shoulders. "When I have seen your mother, I may let you go to her for a few minutes. But you must be very quiet, so as not to excite her. We must avoid anything of an exciting nature. You understand that, don't you, Alice?"

She studied his face which seemed dispassionate. When he held out a hand to her she clung to it desperately and a shudder shook her from head to foot as his hand was so cold.

Letting go of his cold, clammy hand, she said, "Tell me the truth please, is my mother dying?"

He let out a long sigh and said, "Whoever gave you that idea?"

"Ms. Gorham," replied Alice.

He frowned and looked over at the governess. He said nothing, just stared at her.

"She is a governess, not a doctor. I am doing all that can be done to save your mother's life." He then looked directly into Brandy Gorham's eyes with intensity as he said, "Don't worry until I tell you to, and now let me go to see my patient."

The intensity of his glance at the governess as he moved toward Ann Shriver's bedroom was admonishingly direct and penetrating. The demure Alice watched intently as he approached her mother's bedroom door, where he paused a moment, and then softly opened the door and entered while Alice moved to a chair, trembling with concern for her mother, as the governess went back to reading, seemingly unfazed by what was occurring.

The bedroom was bright and cheery, a big room fitted with every luxury imaginable. Upon the bed, beneath a luxurious duvet, lay a woman of forty-one years of age, her beautiful face still fresh and unlined and the deep blue eyes turned pleadingly upon the physician.

The doctor stood by the bedside and said, "I am sorry to keep you waiting. How are you feeling this morning?"

"I do not suffer, but it takes more of the medication to quiet the pain. It is 10 now, and I have taken it four times since midnight," she said with a glance at the nurse who stood silently by the opposite side of the bed.

The doctor nodded, dispassionately looking down at Ann. There was small evidence of illness in her appearance, but he knew that her days were numbered and that death was creeping on with ever increasing assuredness. Ann Shriver knew it, too, and smiled a grim little smile as she added: "How long can I last at this rate?"

"Do not anticipate, Ann," he answered stoically.

"I must know!" she exclaimed. "I have important arrangements to make before my time is up."

Again, dispassionately, he replied, knowing he was lying, "Maybe up to two months. Don't be in a rush."

"You are not honest with me, doctor! What I wish to know is how soon, a concrete how soon. If we manage to defer the end, all the better; but I have several things to get done. I need to summon my attorney from the Huguenot Chambers and get some things finalized."

He seated himself beside the bed and reflected. He knew much about her past life and this was no ordinary woman as her achievements were familiar to many. She was the daughter of Robert Sizemore, whose remarkable career was not known to many in South Africa. He had a faculty for finding gold, but his speculations were invariably unwise, so his constant transitions from affluence to poverty, and vice versa, were extremely frequent. And the last venture of Sizemore, before he died, was to buy the discredited Karoo Tarzana South African mine and develop it.

At that time he was a widower with one motherless child, Ann, a girl of eighteen who had been reared partly in mining camps and partly in her youth at exclusive girls' schools in Switzerland, according to her father's fortunes at any given time. Ann combined culture and refinement with a thorough knowledge of mining obtained at her father's side from the time she was 10, and when her father passed away and left her the Karoo Tarzana mine at only 18, she set to work to make the mine a success, directing her men in person and displaying such shrewd judgment and intelligence, coupled with kindly consideration of the workers, unlike her contemporaries, that she became the idol of the miners, all of whom were proud to be known as employees of the Karoo Tarzana. She was so successful that she sold out at 26 and started a completely unrelated type business, a cosmetics firm that eventually spread all over the world.

Shrewdness in business does not always equate to shrewdness in relationships, as she married an artist named James Shriver, whose talent, it was said, would make a fourth grade artist drawing stick figures think of glory in the art world. His only real claim to fame was being married to his wife. Still, love is often blind, and Ann had no sight at all when judging her husband's art as she saw each one of his paintings as a masterpiece. On her honeymoon, she carried her artist husband to Europe and with him studied the works of the masters in all the art centers of the continent. Then, enthusiastic and eager for his advancement, she returned with him to Johannesburg and set him up in a lavish studio where he had every convenience and incentive to work until she felt he was not living up to his potential and separated from him. The separation led him to be given a very meagre settlement, and the elaborate studio was abandoned and the promising artist disappeared from the Johannesburg public eye, while Ann retained her fortune and control of her business empire, moving to Cape Town. She lived a somewhat secluded life in luxurious hotels all across the world, attending with much solicitude to the training and education of her daughter, Alice, who was apparently of no real interest to her disappeared father.

Alice adored her beautiful mother, and although Ann Shriver was considered sometimes cold and unemotional by those who knew her, there was no doubt she prized her child as her dearest possession and lavished all the tenderness and love of which she was capable upon her.

Retrospectively, Doctor Holcomb thoroughly considered this historical revue of his patient as he sat facing her. It seemed a most unhappy fate that she should be cut off in the flower of her womanhood, but he knew her case was positively hopeless, and he understood it better than anyone realized, and she knew it and had accepted the harsh verdict without a murmur.

"This disease is one that accelerates toward the end," he said. "Within the past few days I have noted its more virulent tendency. All we can do now is to keep you from suffering until the end."

Taking a deep breath and sighing, Ann replied, "And that end will be then in two months?"

"Oh my," offered the doctor. "That would be the absolute most I am afraid."

"Then I must act at once to first make provision for Alice's future, and in this I require your help."

"You can depend on me," he said simply with no emotion in his voice.

"Please contact at once my long-gone husband, James Shriver, in London."

Seemingly unsurprised at the request, he asked, "And where may I find his e-mail address?"

She pointed to a small desk in the far corner of the room. "There, give me the address book from the middle drawer."

He moved slowly toward the desk, removed the book, and almost as if an actor upon the stage of a tragedy unfolding before a rapt audience, he slowly handed her the book, noticing a minute white substance in the right crease of her lips. He reached down, pulled a tissue from the box and gently wiped it away, smelling garlic on her breath, despite the fact she never touched it or allowed it any of her food. He noticed her yellowish complexion, her laboured breathing, even glancing at her skin lesions as he thought the end might well be closer than he anticipated. This was a woman fast approaching that dark pit that will eventually swallow us all.

Looking up at him, she said, "Dr. Holcomb, you have been my good and faithful friend, and you should know why I am now sending for my husband, from whom I have been estranged for many years. When I first met him he was a true artist and I fell in love with his art more than with the man. I desired for him to become a great painter."

Dr. Holcomb sat dispassionately by Ann's bedside as the nurse excused herself. He seemed almost bored by her rendition of a life that she regretted, but she obviously still had fond memories of the time when she found love.

She continued. "He was very poor until he married me, and he had worked industriously to succeed, but as soon as I introduced him to a life of comfort his ambition to work gradually deserted him. With his future provided for, so he thought, he failed to understand the necessity of devoting himself to his brush and palette, but preferred a life of ease, of laziness. So, we quarrelled often over his lack of a work ethic. I tried to force him back to his work, but it was no use; my money had ruined his career. I lost patience and decided to leave him, hoping that when he was back in poverty, he would find that spark of creativity that had deserted him. We were not divorced: we merely separated. Finding I had withdrawn his allowance, he simply was glad to see me go, for he saw me as a bitch that had killed any love he may have had for me. But he loved little Alice, and her loss was difficult. I give him credit for not taking me to court and trying to obtain some of my fortune and to this very day, now twelve years later, has he ever appealed to me for money. I don't know how well he has succeeded, for we never communicate, but I have never heard his name mentioned in any way, anywhere in regards to art, so I assume he has never attained any success in that field. He remained in London as far as I know. A year or two ago I met a man who had known him, and when I asked about what he was doing, the reply was very nebulous with a shake of the head and the very brief mention that he did not know what he did, only that they infrequently ran into one another at a local coffee shop, but he had not seen him in years. Yet, he did recall his e-mail address because it was unusual: lostpicasso@gmail.com. Will you contact him?"

He nodded affirmatively while saying, "What shall I say?"

"Tell him I am dying and seek reconciliation before I pass away. Beg him to come at once as it is an urgent matter for our dear daughter. You must understand that he is an honourable man and in many ways a man of character. I know that he is suited to care for our child and to rear her properly. I have left my entire fortune to Alice, but I have made James my executor, and he is to have control, under certain restrictions, of all the income until Alice is 21. I think he will be glad to accept the responsibility, as he will receive a nice stipend for his time and effort."

"Doubtless, if he has not been a success since your separation, this will be a great boon for him." remarked the doctor.

Lynton and the Cape Town Ghost

"The man I spoke with said he was probably living in near poverty based upon his shabby appearance. He indicated that although he had succeeded in selling a few paintings they had brought rather insignificant sums. I may well be mistaken in thinking his talent exceptional, as it was probably based more on an assessment of my love than his talent. Anyhow, my experiment in leaving him to his own devices seems not to have resulted as I had hoped, and I now am willing that he should handle Alice's income for the next few years and live very comfortably while she matures into adulthood. It is likely that she will provide for her father when she comes of age, and I have not included such a request in my will but I have endeavoured, in case he proves inclined to neglect her, to require the court to appoint another guardian, but I know this will not happen. That is because I know his nature is gentle and kind, and he adores, or at least he used to sincerely adore, Alice."

The doctor sat, as he accepted the notebook, turned to the page with Shriver's e-mail address, into his outstretched hand. His dispassionate demeanour seemed to fade as there was a slight twinkle in his eyes. The matter-of-fact way in which she referred to her marital relations and her assumed unconcern over her own dreadful fate was impressive he thought.

Shriver's failure to succeed as an artist, while it might have been a source of discontent to his art-loving wife, did not seem to matter to Dr.

Holcomb one way or another. He could not help but ask, "Does dear Alice even know her father?"

"She was only two years old when we separated."

"And you say your will is finalized?"

"Armand Hardy, my lawyer, has attended to it. It is now in his possession, properly signed and witnessed."

"If Hardy drew the will, it is doubtless legal and in accordance with your wishes. But who witnessed it? It must be witnessed by more than just your lawyer."

"Your nurse, Jane, witnessed it this very day," she said as Jane Arnold, walked back into the room.

The doctor glanced at the fine figure of woman, who stood by the window perfectly motionless, her eyes meeting the doctor's. She was a young woman, maybe around thirty, and the nurse's uniform could not hide her shapeliness. She displayed a certain cockiness in her demeanour, as if she was attractive and knew it. Dr. Holcomb found himself admiring her fine frame and piercing eyes. He had recommended the woman to Ann Shriver, having frequently employed her on other cases and found her highly skilful and reliable. Her signature to the will he regarded as satisfactory in case any problems arouse.

A moan from Ann suddenly aroused the doctor. Her face was beginning to tremble spasmodically with pain. In an instant Nurse Jane was at her side, hypodermic needle in hand, and the opiate was soon administered with the doctor nodding his approval. Opiates are both a scourge and a blessing thought Dr. Holcomb. He was so right, but which was it for dear Ann? Could it be both?

The doctor eased toward the door as he said, "I will send Alice in, as she desperately wants to see you, but do not exert yourself. Only a few minutes, please."

"Of course," replied Ann. She then, with great conviction, said, "Don't forget to contact dear James. I cannot rest in peace until I know he is coming to his daughter's side."

The child crept softly to her mother's bedside, but once there she impulsively threw her arms about Ann's neck and embraced her so tightly that the sick woman was obliged to push her arms away. She did this tenderly, though, and kissed both of Alice's cheeks before she said, "I've news for you, dear."

Hope springing forth in the heart of Alice, she, in a delightful voice, said, "Are you better Mommy?"

"Honestly dear, no I am not. Some people simply are prone to an early death, and I must prepare you for the worst. Your mommy must leave you soon."

Eyes filling with tears, Alice fell upon her mother's chest as Ann continued. "You must not expect mamma ever to get well, my darling. But that shouldn't worry you—not too much. You know one of the queer things about life is that it has an end, sooner or later, and in mamma's case it comes to an end a little sooner than you and I might wish it to. I am not sorry for myself, but for you, because you and I are so close, but you are going to be taken care of."

As poor Alice sobbed, Ann, in an almost whisper, said, "You are in for a grand surprise darling, as your father, who loved you devotedly when you were a baby, but whom you have never known since I left him, is coming here to see us soon."

Alice's heart began to pump faster but it was not because of the news about her long gone father, but because she was reticent to face the reality that her mother was going to die. She pleaded with her mother. "Don't mamma. Please don't leave me. I cannot face life without you."

Taking a deep breath and sighing, Ann, with deep emotion, her voice trembling, said, "Had I any command over life and death, my darling daughter, I would never leave you, because you are my entire life. When it is too late to help it, we realize what is really important in our lives. When it is too late to change things, we realize that death has knocked on our door, and the time has simply passed when we can make a change. Thus is the fate of all humanity? I should have reached out to your father before now, made sure he came to see you, but I was selfish, wanting you all to myself. You will love your father, because he is good, and because he will want to do the right thing by you. He is a fine man, and kindly, so I believe he will make your life as happy as I could have done. He will be by your side just as I have been. He will look out for your welfare, because you are his flesh and blood. You will be loved as much by him as you have been by me."

"I don't want him. I need you mamma! It is you I need more than anything else in the world," she sobbed uncontrollably as a dispassionate Nurse Arnold stood by the window, looking out onto the waterfront mall.

Nurse Arnold turned and advanced toward the bed, where Alice lay sobbing in her mother's arms and whispered, "Control yourself, dear. You must be brave and not upset your mother; otherwise, I shall have to ask you to leave."

Getting control of her emotions, Alice looked up at her mother and said, "Tell me dear mother, what am I to do?"

It was thus, with fading breath that Ann Shriver, a dying woman, spoke not of herself but of Alice's father and of how she expected her to conduct herself while she grew into womanhood. She spoke of her will, and how under the direction of her father, it meant her interests would always be protected. To this Alice listened intently and, although she still trembled at times, she was determined to cry no more and face the reality of the situation with stoic dedication to letting her mother know she had a daughter who would be steadfast and not waver before adversity. Dimly she realized that her mother was suffering through the knowledge of their inevitable parting and felt she could comfort her beloved mother more by controlling her grief bravely than by giving way to it in her mother's presence.

Meantime, Doctor Holcomb had returned to his office and had very carefully written and dispatched the following e-mail:

lostpicasso@gmail.com

Your wife is dying at the Belvedere Hotel in Cape Town and wishes reconciliation before she passes away. Come quickly, as any delay may prove dangerous. Notify me when to expect you.
Sincerely,
Rob

The next morning he told Ann Shriver that he had received a very quick reply to his e-mail that said, "I shall come immediately but have no funds for the trip."

He showed Ann the printed response he brought with him, but it had no place of origin and her eyes glistened with concern as she said, "Any decent man would have borrowed the money, or even pawned his watch and jewellery to get to a dying wife who calls for him. I hope I am not mistaken in his continued kindly character. Yet, I am sure he has not changed; only perhaps he is just still trapped in a desperate financial situation. Send him whatever he needs and bill me."

Holcomb did not hesitate going to the local Western Union and sending money, furnishing the required sum from his own pocket. He even sent more than was necessary, muttering to himself: "This is an investment that will raise this man from poverty to affluence, for little Alice's income will be enormous and he has seven years before her 21st birthday, at least, to enjoy it unrestrained, or maybe he will wind up with it all one day."

It was Ann's trust in James Shriver that was going to lead eventually to Lynton Viñas' involvement in this whole sordid affair. Ann was putting trust in someone she had not seen in twelve years. For a smart businesswoman, she was throwing caution to the wind and through concern for her daughter's welfare, perhaps leaving some stones unturned that should have been rolled over and thoroughly examined.

Ann was visibly excited when she received from the doctor a copy of an e-mail that read: *I will arrive tomorrow night at 9:00 PM your time. Looking forward to seeing you.* She turned to the doctor and said, "You need to be here, if you can please, so that you can meet with him first and prepare him for the worst, because even though we have practically been strangers for years, he is sure to be grieved and sympathetic. But do not bore him with particulars. Send him to me as soon as you have prepared him."

Looking around the room, Doctor Robert Holcomb seemed to be momentarily distracted. He peered out the window at the gathering clouds in the far distance. The Cape of Good Hope's famous penchant for stirring fierce winds that accompany storms would surely prevail on this day. Was it a precursor of stern winds of adversity that would soon swell about in the lives of those gathered there on this day? Would carnage ensue? The trees outside were writhing and flailing, their groans of pain carried away by the wind. Would the storm scream like a banshee, uprooting weeds and shrubs in a fit of ever-consuming rage? Would pounding rain hammer the ground like an impenetrable salvo of bullets? Livid black clouds were rearing up like a cobra readying itself for attack. Suddenly, lightning mercilessly spit out its bright venom from those dark clouds in the distance. Ann heard the clamouring thunder and sighed.

Ann was filled with a sense of foreboding as her eyes locked on Doctor Holcomb. There was a darkness descending on the room. Ann feared that unless James Shriver arrived soon that darkness might creep outward and also embrace her daughter in its malevolence.

Chapter 2
Doubting Sanity

A man sauntered into the opulent lobby of the Belvedere Grand Hotel, looking around in awe at the splendour of the place. A bellboy hastened to relieve him of his luggage, which was one brown canvas bag strapped with a cord. This man was very plainly dressed. His clothing slightly tattered, worn shabbily. He had on a grey shirt with an open collar. His light brown pants were a bit weather-stained. His shoes were shabby and un-shined. He wore no socks. His appearance was out of keeping with the palatial hotel he had just entered, where he was getting stares from the bombastic rich who always look down on the less fortunate, as an offence to their eyes.

Lynton and the Cape Town Ghost

Without relinquishing his baggage to the bellboy, he asked sharply, "Is a Doctor Holcomb hereabouts?"

Doctor Holcomb, who had been impatiently waiting, spied the arrival, and after a cursory scan up and down of the shabbily dressed man, leaped from his nearby chair and said in a loud tone, almost as if he wanted to make sure everyone heard him, "Mr. Shriver, I assume?"

Equally loud, the man replied, "Doctor Holcomb, the man who e-mailed me?"

"I am indeed."

Very curtly, Shriver said, "Take me to my wife immediately, please."

There was no sentimentality to his tone, which was slow and distinct and very sharp. He seemed ill at ease and looked around the lobby, as if fearing he had entered the wrong place.

The doctor said, "I will lead you to her presently but first I must acquaint you with her condition, which is serious. I have engaged a room for you here, and if you will please register, then we will go into the bar and talk."

"All right," replied Shriver as he registered at the desk while all those in the lobby stared at him with obvious disdain while he was registering. As the twenty or so people in the lobby cast curious glances at him, he headed into the bar with Holcomb. The bellboy followed with his bag he now had been handed. They took a seat, not in some secluded corner, but right in the centre of the room. The grandeur of the room they entered seemed not to astonish the artist. He made no remark but slowly seated himself and looked inquiringly at Doctor Holcomb. The bellboy put down the bag in a vacant chair and the doctor handed him a twenty rand tip.

"Ms. Shriver," began the doctor, "is dying as I alluded to in our last communiqué. I cannot say how long she may survive, but it is a matter of days, perhaps even hours. Her greatest anxiety at present is to be reconciled with you, whom she has not seen or even communicated with for years."

As they talked, the people around them could easily overhear what was being said. They were all witnesses to the strange story unfolding in the luxurious bar. A waiter came over and the two men ordered tea.

Very loudly, Shriver said, "She really wants to reconcile then? She actually told you that?"

"She did, yes."

"Rather an unusual idea after all these years." remarked Mr. Shriver, musingly.

"Very natural, I think, under the circumstances," stoically replied the doctor. "She has every confidence in you and admires your character exceedingly, although it was her desire that you live apart all these years. She only speaks highly of you on every occasion."

Shriver's stolid countenance relaxed in a slow grin as he glanced around the room and those listening purposefully bowed their heads or looked away to feign disinterest in the conversation. Shriver was an average height man who was thin of figure and hardened of muscle. He took a deep breath and sighed. His head was bald in front, giving him the appearance of a high forehead, and the hair at the back and around the ears was beginning to grey. His eyes were light blue; his nose was broad and his jaws prominent. His age was about forty-five, near that of Ann Shriver.

"Ann," continued the doctor, "knows that you are due to arrive at this time and is eagerly counting the minutes, because she has important business matters to arrange with you before she passes away."

"Business matters?"

"So she has told me," the doctor said, after a brief period of hesitation that seemed contrived, during which he noticed the bellboy standing attentively by the arched entrance to the bar, seemingly straining his ears to hear what was being said by the two men, as did the waiter who brought tea.

"I will allow you to see your wife at once that you may learn her plans from her own lips."

The change of James Shriver in the intervening years had perhaps been very extreme; as it was obvious he had probably led such a difficult life that his self esteem had been sorely strained if not broken. Shriver seemed to contrive showing he was overwhelmed. Was he wondering if Ann would revise her opinion of him and make other disposition of her finances and the guardianship of her child when she got a good look at him and took his measure? Would she even recognize him?

Lynton and the Cape Town Ghost

The doctor looked over at the bellboy as the two men took a last gulp of their tea and signalled for him to come back to the table where he picked up the bag as Doctor Holcomb placed 200 Rand on the table, which included a generous tip.

Without any further remark the two got up and went to Shriver's room where the bag was deposited. The doctor tipped the boy, who turned and scurried out. The two proceeded down the hall to Ann's penthouse elevator at the end of the floor. The governess had been instructed to take Alice for a stroll; thereby, there was no one in the little reception room. Here, however, the doctor halted, and pointing to the door at the further end of the passage, he said, "That is your wife's bedroom. Please enter quietly and remember the danger of exciting her unduly. Be gentle and considerate." For some reason, he then looked around to see if someone might be lurking about unseen.

Shriver actually smiled at the doctor, winked and moved toward the bedroom. For a moment he regarded the door with curious intentness, seemingly reluctant to turn the knob. Then he slowly opened it and went in, closing the door softly behind him.

Dr. Holcomb seated himself in the reception room, looking around it as if he felt an unknown presence. He even looked at the floor which was darkened now by closed curtains. He found himself curiously gazing down, as if expecting to see a pair of shoes sticking out beneath the closed curtains. Why was he so suspicious?

Lynton and the Cape Town Ghost

Meanwhile, the puzzled looking artist moved toward the sleeping Ann Shriver with soft, purposeful strides. This summons to his dying-wife was not really a surprise based upon the slight smirk on his face. Yet, the man appeared, at the same time, dazed and even bewildered by the event, and while he had once lived in luxurious surroundings his later experiences must have been so wholly different that the splendour of his wife's mode of living made him temporarily shake his head from side to side in confusion. Yes, the contrast to the way he supposedly lived was stark. He had formerly shared Ann's immense wealth; he had enjoyed the finest studio in all South Africa; and then in the blink of an eye he was back to poverty, stuck in drudgery, struggling for mere existence. Years of hardship were likely to have had a decided effect upon the character of a man who was doubtless weak in the beginning. It could have made him hard and bitter, and as he moved beside her bed, there was resentment etched on his face, or was it more than that. There was a curious smile slowly rippling across his lips as he gazed down at the woman on the bed almost as if she were a complete stranger.

As the doctor sat quietly, still suspecting a presence in the reception room, a sudden shrill voice broke through the silence with a scream. Dr. Holcomb sprang to his feet and hurried into the patient's bedroom, where Shriver was standing and staring in disbelief. His emotion was obviously not love but surprise.

Lynton and the Cape Town Ghost

The physician hastened to the bedside, where Jane Arnold, the nurse, was bending over the stilled form of Ann. She held a pillow in her hand as the doctor looked down at Ann Shriver.

The woman was dead. At the very moment of reunion with the husband from whom she had so long been parted, she had moved into the death realm, leaving reconciliation in abeyance. She had a look of profound shock on her face.

The body lay beneath the duvet with features contorted, mouth half open and eyes staring wildly. A paroxysm of pain had carried her off it would be assumed; the pain, and the excitement of the moment when she saw a familiar face from the past had caused shock. Seeing James Shriver had simply been too much for her when she opened her eyes and saw him standing there by her bed.

Very deliberately he bent down, closed the eyes and pressed the lips ever so gently together. He purposefully smoothed the lines from the bright red cheeks, so that the face became more natural in appearance and with his right index finger he gently wiped the white residue that had so often appeared on the left or right crease of her lips. Then, with a sigh, he turned away to find Shriver and the nurse confronting one another in tense attitudes, hugging each other with compassion. Shriver stared wonderingly into the nurse's face. Jane, her eyes now riveted on Shriver, returned the stare with an expression that belied description. Suddenly, all three were staring at one another without any expression of sadness, but of recognition that the suddenness of the death was so apparently unexpected, or was it?

Jane turned her back abruptly, while Shriver swung around and tiptoed hastily from the room. His shoulders stooped as he exited, as if there was the unbearable weight of worry upon them.

The doctor stopped in the doorway, looked at the nurse reflectively and asked, "Who was it that screamed? Was it you?"

She hesitated a moment. "It was I," she replied. "I saw her face and knew that the end had come."

It was a lie, and the nurse knew that the shrewd doctor recognized it as a lie. Anyway, as they looked at one another with intensity, it seemed not to matter why there had been a scream. The doctor made a last intense look toward the bed as he left the room with an admonition to the nurse, "Do not touch the body."

Time soothes all wounds of the heart. The scars remain, perhaps, but as the clock ticks on the ache is stilled and the soreness finally passes away. At first, Alice was heart-broken over her mother's loss. She lived in a sort of stupor for weeks after the private funeral. Her father's presence she accepted without comment or emotion, for it had been arranged by her loving mother. She did not consider, in those first weeks, whether she cared for her newly found father or not. Her mother's statement that he was a good man and would love her dearly was taken by the adolescent as a matter of fact, while her mother's injunction to love him and confide in him was ignored.

Lynton and the Cape Town Ghost

The will had been read in Alice's presence, and although Ann had wanted to enter stipulations into the document, there were none added due to the suddenness of her death. Alice simply accepted things as they were, but those first weeks her new protector was rarely seen, as James Shriver retained his separate room at the hotel and allowed Alice and her governess to inhabit the grand suite her mother had occupied. Ann's room was closed and the curtains drawn, but every night before she retired to her own little room Alice would sullenly meander into the dark, depressing bedroom and feel her way to the lonely empty bed and gently kiss the pillow on which her mother's head had rested. She would then, with heavy heart, sob uncontrollably into that pillow, leaving it moist with her tears.

Brandy Gorham, the governess, was aware of these evening excursions, but offered no objection. Indeed, the woman objected to nothing that did not interfere with her own personal comfort and convenience. Under the eyes of Ann, she had been prim and dutiful, but there was no one to chide her now no matter how neglectful she chose to be, and it was true that during these days Alice required no particular care as she resumed her morning studies with meekness a week after her mother had been buried. She was dealing with her mother's death in an almost zombie-like state, simply existing with no real life within, only robotic indifference to her surroundings and those with whom she came in contact.

Lynton and the Cape Town Ghost

Despite her highly reserved nature, Ann had accumulated a wide circle of acquaintances who sincerely mourned her extremely untimely death and would have been glad to befriend Alice, but her highly secretive father was guarding her welfare with a seemingly complete dedication to isolating her from everyone. The few of her mother's acquaintances she did encounter seemed to sadden her state deeper as she listened to their unanimous praise of her dear departed mother, making her realize in sombre loneliness the depth of her loss.

Her father was never present on these occasions. He was by no means a sociable man. Sometimes he came in for a few minutes in the morning, and sat down to stare at the girl in a way half curious and half speculative manner, said little, and presently went away as quietly as he had come. Meanwhile, Nurse Arnold had left on the day that Ann died, and Alice had almost forgotten the young woman when one afternoon she came to see her when walking with Brandy Gorham. Nurse Arnold no longer wore her uniform but was dressed in ultra-fashionable apparel, and to Alice's amusement, displayed the manners of a sophisticated, well-bred lady. She talked more with Brandy than with Alice and was keen to know what arrangements had been made for the future. Miss Gorham admitted that she had no idea of Mr. Shriver's intentions. Of course they could not remain long in the elaborate hotel suite, a smaller one would be more satisfactory in every way, but Mr. Shriver had not as yet mentioned the subject.

A few days afterward, during one of her walks along Waterfront Street with Brandy Gorham, Alice was surprised to see her father and Nurse Arnold riding past in an auto being driven by Nurse Arnold. The two seemed to be engaged in frantic conversation and neither noticed Alice or Brandy Gorham. Brandy must have also noticed them, as Alice observed her rather disdainful look, but neither of them made any comment.

Letters of executor-ship had been issued to James and the control of his daughter's property legally placed in his hands. Attorney Armand Hardy attended to all the necessary details, and appeared to have a real personal affinity for James Shriver and his suitability for the task of handling so much money and a myriad of assets. Thereby, he loyally and with great dedication persisted in seeing that the dead woman's wishes be obeyed to the letter.

Several of Ann's friends had been to personally see the lawyer about severe misgivings concerning Shriver, pleading that Alice was likely to suffer through the man's indifference and lack of credibility, but Hardy declared it was not his duty to criticize the man's character but to see that the wishes of his clients were obeyed. He intonated that in this case, doubtless the man's wife knew him more intimately than anyone else and if she trusted him, aware as she must have been of his faults and virtues, it would be presumptuous for anyone to try to break her will or otherwise interfere with her carefully planned arrangements.

Through it all, there was a bit of outwardly change in James Shriver. He had bought new clothes and trimmed his unruly hair, and although he did not wear the clothes with any air of superiority as did most rich people in their finery, he did cut a far more dashing appearance. He was quiet and unassuming; he made no friends and few acquaintances; he never mentioned himself or his personal history and never referred to his wife except when forced to do so by those of her acquaintances that came by on occasion to check on Alice. All these people found him so unresponsive that they soon left him alone and came back no more.

The legal business, even though it progressed smoothly, required time for consummation, so it was somewhat more than four months before all the details were complete. Alice, a sadly despondent child with no special interest in life, kept no track of time and plodded along in her tutored studies and never ventured out of the penthouse except for her daily walks, which were every bit as sad as staying in the hotel, because all she did was ponder on the times she used to stroll the same haunts with her beloved mother. Hers was a dismal existence.

Then, one morning James came into the quarters and without any emotion simply said to Alice and Governess Gorham, "Pack up right now. We are outta here."

"What do you mean, sir?" retorted a seemingly surprised Brandy Gorham.

"Just what I said! Get Alice's things and your own ready immediately to move out of this place right away. Also pack the personal belongings of Ms. Shriver. Put them in separate trunks and boxes, so I can easily dispose of them. Do you understand me?"

"Yes, sir."

Alice listened with intensity, but said nothing, for what choice had she but to do as ordered by her father? However, eventually her curiosity got the best of her as she said, "Where are we going?"

Miss Gorham, for some reason, appeared uninterested, as Shriver looked at her and winked, turned and left the room without reply.

Three days was little enough time to gather up and pack all the things that had been accumulated over the years. The governess knew there were many big trunks in the storeroom of the hotel, and these she ordered brought up to the rooms. Then she procured two maids, told them what and how to pack, and composedly sat down nonchalantly in her favourite chair and read while the others worked furiously to meet the deadline for moving. All this time, there was not even one appearance by James Shriver.

When Alice asked her how she could sit and read while others worked so diligently, she replied, "I am not one hired to do manual labour. I am hired to tutor you in academics and to teach you the refinement of being a lady."

Alice thought that she was now growing in a strong dislike for her governess who thought herself better than others. Despite her mother's wealth, she had always taught Alice to respect all those who had to toil in obscurity for their daily bread.

Finally, James Shriver made an appearance one morning. "Is everything ready?" he demanded.

Gorham declared that she had worked extra hard to see all was properly packed, much to the chagrin of Alice who was appalled by her taking credit for what others had done.

Gorham asked, "And where are we going?"

Then, Alice got a bit of pleasure at seeing what happened next, as it was befitting that someone so arrogant be put in her place as Shriver replied, "You are going wherever you please. Your services are no longer required."

"You're going to fire me?" she said.

"You got that right missy."

"But who will look after Alice? She needs a tutor and a comforter when she is low in spirits."

"I will." He said abruptly as he extended his hand filled with several thousand Rand, continuing with no compassion in his voice. "Here is your money. I have paid you one month in advance in lieu of notice."

"A month? I'm hired by the year," asserted the woman defiantly, but her protestations seemed contrived, almost as if it was an act.

"Have you a written contract?"

"No; a verbal contract is just as good."

"Maybe and maybe not. See you in court if you desire, and we'll let a judge decide. Now, go please." He, too, seemed to be performing.

The governess looked at him with what again appeared contrived disbelief, almost as if she was an actor in a stage play. Why wondered Alice?

Alice, never fond of her governess, regarded the dismissal with as much unconcern as her father displayed. Brandy Gorham had been her companion for years, but had never won the smallest corner of the girl's genuinely tender heart. Although she was not aware of the fact, the woman's constant presence and lack of interest in her welfare had always been a barrier to any simpatico they might have had. Thus, Alice's first sensation, on realizing their future separation, was one of distinct relief.

As Brandy Gorham departed, she looked over at her pupil with piercing eyes, but said nothing. She simply walked out.

Alice's father abruptly turned to her and very curtly said, "Come," as he walked toward the door.

She followed him to a waiting taxicab, in which had been heaped her hand luggage and his own, and they drove away from the grand hotel where she had lived in luxury for so long, and where so many indelible memories had been impressed upon her mind, with as little ado as if they had been transient guests.

When the cab pulled up at the airport, Alice asked: "Are we leaving town father?'

"Yes," he replied; "I am returning with you to London."

She felt a slight sinking of the heart as she realized that the old life, in which her adored and beloved mother had played so prominent a part, was being abandoned forever, and this deeply troubled her.

Still, she felt a tinge of elation as since her mother had died the old life had lost its charm and become dull, mundane and stupid. Alice was not sure she could be happier elsewhere, but her crushed and dispirited nature responded to the suggestion of change. It was interesting to have something different to look forward to. Still, if only her father was more affectionate she thought, then it would be easier to embrace a new life, but the man beside her in the cab was no more congenial than Gorham had been, but he was her father; he was the guardian selected by her dear mother, and in obeying his wishes she might find her future life more pleasurable than had been the dreadful dreary months since her mother had left her.

Somehow, James Shriver seemed uneasy in the presence of his daughter. The young girl was equally uncomfortable in her father's presence and was well pleased to be left so much alone. So, with very little questioning or conversation on either side, father and daughter maintained an emotional detachment. Alice found herself deposited in a small suite of rooms on the third floor of a grimy and dingy flat near Piccadilly

Lynton and the Cape Town Ghost

Square in central London. There were several little tin signs nailed beside the entrance and Alice noticed that one of them read: *James Shriver Studio – 3rd Floor*. It was a newer sign, but scarcely legible, while others beside it seemed older, and when the girl had climbed laboriously up the three flights and the artist had unlocked the door at the head of the stairs with a key which he took from his pocket, she found everything about the rooms to appear purposefully made to look old. This then, she thought, must have been his home and studio for many years before he came scurrying to Cape Town at the behest of her mother. He was more than just a failed artist. He was a failed father as well she proposed in her mind that was now racing with doubt about what lay ahead for her in this most dreary of places.

The fact that it was beginning to grow dark prevented Alice from more than a cursory observation of the obvious tawdriness of her new home. However, what she saw inspired her more with curiosity than dismay. She had been reared in an atmosphere of luxury that bestowed upon her a sense of being an aristocrat, but she never slighted those less fortunate than she, nor looked with disdain upon those who, through the circumstances of a world based on greed, were subject to always being on the outside looking in. She understood that most people did not live the privileged life she had.

Ironically, the very fact that her father's humble flat was different made it far more interesting to the adolescent than new apartments such as she had been accustomed to. Therefore she had no thought, at that time, of protest. Her own little room contained a small iron bed, one straight chair and a broken-legged dresser over which hung a cracked mirror. The small wool rug was worn threadbare and needed vacuuming.

While she stood in the doorway of her room, solemnly regarding it, her father said over her shoulder, "You won't need both those big trunks here, I'm sure. I'll store them somewhere in the studio. Covered with drapes, they won't be noticed. I can't imagine why that horrible woman packed so much. She should have given some items away. You do not need all this."

Without hesitation, Alice interjected, "That will not be nearly enough. Why Ms. Gorham was about to engage a dressmaker for me when you whisked me away. I am used to a vast wardrobe."

"Then we moved just in time to save that expense," he declared, setting his stern jaws together. "There's been a terrible waste of money through that woman Gorham. We're well rid of that cranky old witch."

He looked over at a rickety old desk and said, "You can hook up your computer on that. I'll arrange for internet tomorrow."

He turned away toward the studio and Alice followed him there. She took a look at the workroom and thought it seemed more comfortable than the other rooms of the flat. Her father began dusting and arranging half a dozen paintings of various sizes, mounted on stretchers. None was finished; some were scarcely begun. All appeared freshly painted. She tried to see what they represented. Perhaps she had inherited a bit of artistic instinct; if so, it was that which prompted her to shrug her small shoulders slightly and then turn away to the window. In the dimly lit street outside, a man drove up with the other baggage. Shriver had purchased for himself new trunks, a small one and a big expensive one, and there were two big trunks and a suitcase belonging to Alice. After these had been carried up and placed in the studio, her father said, "We will go out now and get some dinner."

Alice marvelled at the restaurant even more than at the dingy studio she had observed earlier. It looked old, dilapidated and, above all, extremely dirty. It was filled with people who had glazed looks of hopelessness. No doubt, it was fitting for this particular area of Piccadilly, an area of poverty amongst plenty, but that was the way of a United Kingdom that had, like America, lost its way in the 1980's when the Ronald Reagan of the U.K., Margaret Thatcher, had also introduced with glee the culture of greed. Those two had destroyed unions, and along with them, the last hope for working men and women to get economic justice. The entire world had embraced the culture of greed, even China, where communism was now nothing but a word, just as democracy was no more than just a word in the USA. It was a word that connotated freedom, but there was no freedom when one single human being languished in poverty while others lived in luxurious opulence. The irony was the very people who struggled for survival each day would dutifully line up to wave and cheer the royal leeches who paraded by in gold encrusted carriages.

When they sat down, a man with a blood stained apron and a dirty rag in his right hand sauntered over to their table, and bending low, whispered in Shriver's ear, "You know James I must have cash up front for your meal. I simply cannot afford to carry you anymore."

"Of course," replied Alice's father, with a slight frown. "In fact, bring my previous bill and I will settle it now."

He not only, to the surprise of the man, settled his previous bill, but also included a generous tip. During the meal, James Shriver cast frequent puzzled glances into the face of his daughter, who until now had accepted her changed conditions with evident indifference. As they ate together in complete silence, Alice's demure features grew grave-like and thoughtful. Her father shrank from meeting the inquiring glances of her big eyes. Yet, not once since first laying eyes on him had she dared question him in any way. She simply accepted what he told her to do without complaint. Still, the grave look upon her face was obviously puzzling James.

After dinner they went back to the dingy studio, where James picked up a paper and sat across from his daughter who was staring at him. They were both reserved. There was an indefinable barrier between them, which each was beginning to intensely recognize.

Alice sighed deeply and asked to go to bed and he sent her away with a nod of relief, saying, "Please do that."

Next morning they had breakfast at the same dingy little café, and afterward Alice unpacked some things, putting them in the broken dresser. It seemed odd to have no maid to do it for her, but she was not one to ever think she was too good to do menial manual labour. As she passed to and from the outer studio several times retrieving items, she noticed that her father was staring, with a shocked look on his face, at a painting depicting a large vial in the hands of a lady with long, almost witch-like nails. Her face was covered by a black veil, but it was transparent enough to see she had a sinister look as she was moving toward a beautiful woman lying on the grass by a meandering stream. He was painstakingly studying the painting and never raised or turned his head when Alice walked into the room. It was as if he was transfixed only on his painting, which, to the untrained eye of Alice, seemed mediocre at best. His intense staring at the canvas appeared to indicate a complete lack of confidence in his ability. Alice stopped and looked at the painting and her father was visibly shaking. He had no reaction to her, as he simply stared at his work, as if he, too, knew it was a lacklustre effort. Still, the two said nothing.

Lynton and the Cape Town Ghost

Alice plodded drearily along in her new life for several days. Then, she began to grow restless, for the place was repulsive to her. As she sat squirming with misery at her lot in life, staring at her father and that infernal painting, an unusual incident occurred that would light the flame of curiosity.

One day the door opened and a woman walked into the studio. Her body swayed gently and seductively into the room, being for all things amorously fashioned as if she were ivory on a polished piano keyboard that played tunes of sensuality. The immaculate crisp head was under flowing locks that cascaded over her dainty shoulders. Upon a keen and delicately soft face a beautiful strangeness floated like a stately ship bounding over undulating waves in the open ocean. Her eyes twinkled with deadliness, as if she might be a cobra ready to strike. Her lips were slightly parted, full and painted as red as a bullfighter's cape. She stood tall and ram-rod erect, displaying a confident demeanour in her highly fashionable attire that projected an extreme air of sophistication. Her clinging, silken dress appeared to have been spun by worms that must have died in glory realizing their work would grace the body of such a beautiful creature. She was somewhat too alluring for daytime good taste, for her cleavage displayed generous breasts that were obviously of the man-made variety. Adding to the dichotomy, she wore considerable jewellery, including diamonds; her shoes were elegant and obviously hand-made by a cobbler of considerable skill. If good clothes could make a lady, there was no question of her social standing. Yet, Alice felt this woman was out of her element, and that she fell short in some vague way of being what she was ambitious to appear. The woman was none other than Nurse Jane Arnold!

Jane Arnold very sternly and intensely looked the room up and down, glanced at Alice without a word, only a measured stare. She then turned to James and said with apparent contempt, "So, this is where the next Rembrandt paints his masterpieces."

Alice's father confronted the woman with a menacing frown. "What do you mean by coming here?"

"I am here for two reasons," she said with a sarcastic tone. Then, with a near laugh, continued, "I simply wanted to see how such a rich man lives. And, I must say, I am not impressed."

Without any equivocation, he replied, as he eased into a chair near that infernal painting, "Well, you can see that money has not altered my pedestrian tastes."

"I certainly do see that, and I realize you are quite comfortable and ought to be happy here," she offered as she looked at Alice, "with the millionaire heiress."

Alice met her look with disconcerting gravity, her eyes expressing wonderment at the unfolding event that was playing out in the dingy studio where her father wrapped himself in his own little world as that one work of art before him seemed to trump all other worldly considerations, an artwork in Alice's opinion that was lacking in any credible hope for acceptance by the public.

"Your sneers and your opulent mode of dress, along with your newly acquired expensive generous womanly assets," said James, still frowning but now speaking with composure, "must indicate that you erroneously consider yourself freed from any and all servitude. I do not see that my mode of living is any of your business, Jane. You would do well to show less affluence at this time. It is simply not wise to show any affluence. Showing too much wealth too soon is not prudent in our circumstances."

"It is easier to be content when you have a fortune at your disposal. You do not worry where your next meal might come from," and then she turned to look directly at Alice, "thanks to little missy here."

She took a seat on the worn, dilapidated sofa as if it were a crate in a junk yard, being careful not to muss her elegant dress, smoothing it out as she sat. Cynically smiling, she said, "Now for the reason I came here from South Africa." Slowly and smoothly passing her hand over her upper body, she continued, "All this is costly, so I want some money. No, I demand some money."

Tilting his head down, James sarcastically said, "What took you so long?"

"Don't be sarcastic with me! I want it now, and lots of it, as promised."

Her ruby red lips seemed to be ablaze, as she separated them, displaying glistening white teeth, blurting out, "Don't trifle with me. You cannot afford to anger me."

James wiggled in his seat, took a deep breath and looked over at Alice, then back at Jane. "This is neither the time, the place or in the right company to brooch this subject. I am appalled that you would even consider doing this. It is highly inappropriate here and now."

"You are a miserly coward who will be exposed, if I do not get my just deserts. Don't you realize you can pay high rent now and eat three expensive meals a day, and not have to work and slave for them? You have life made for many, many years." Then she looked directly at Alice, actually pointing her finger gingerly at the girl, as she continued, "Maybe even far longer if certain circumstances materialize. That girl is your pot of gold, that little missy is your diamond mine, your gold mine, your silver mine, your ticket on the leisure train."

James glanced uneasily at Alice, almost seeming to want her sympathy for enduring the tirade from Jane Arnold. A slight crooked grin creased his lips as he said to Jane Arnold, "Owing to my dead wife's generosity, you are right. My daughter and I are both fortunate."

Jane's demeanour was sinister, with eyes glaring intensely, seeming to sear James' flesh like he was nude in a hail storm, where every chunk of falling ice was a frosted dagger sharply cutting his skin.

She spit out words like arrows springing forth from a taunt bow. "Of course, if you play your cards right, little missy here will take care of daddy forever. And why? Because you happen to be a master manipulator, and for that simple reason you are now reaping great rewards, because you had the good fortune for an emotional and stupid woman to die young and put you in charge of her estate and her poor orphaned child here who may actually believe you are concerned about her welfare. So, for goodness sake, don't grumble about writing me a check."

All this was frankly said in the presence of Alice, whose person and fortune her father was now sole guardian. It was understandable that the man seemed annoyed and ill at ease. His scowl grew darker and his eyes glinted in an ugly way as he replied, after a brief pause, "I have a duty to Alice. I take that duty seriously. She will not keep a huge staff of servants it's true, as a simple life is best for her. She'll grow up a more sensible and competent woman by waiting on herself and living as most girls do."

Displaying a calmer demeanour, Jane Arnold said, "Alice has been spoiled, and a bit of worldly experience will do her good. One day, yes, she will be very rich, when she comes into her fortune, and then she can do as she likes with her money. Just now her income is too big for her needs, and the best thing you can do is to teach her economy, a virtue you have refined out of an orchestrated plan. However, all that is irrelevant. I came for a check and I expect it. Others have received theirs, and I expect mine here and now."

James arose, walked over to a desk in the corner and removed a check book from a drawer. Alice, although she had listened intently to the astonishing conversation, did not quite comprehend what it meant. Jane's harsh statement bewildered her as much as did her father's subservience to the woman. All she realized was that Jane Arnold, her dead mother's nurse, wanted money and her father was reluctant to give it to her but dared not refuse. Money was an abstract quantity to the adolescent; she had never handled it personally and knew nothing of its value. If her father owed Jane some money, perhaps it was for back wages, or services rendered her mother, and Alice was annoyed that he haggled about it, even though the woman evidently demanded more than was just. There was plenty of money, she believed, and it was undignified to argue with a former servant who was obviously owed compensation.

James wrote the check and handed it to Jane. "There, that squares our account. It is what I agreed to give you, but I did not think you would demand it so soon. To pay it just now leaves me in an untenable position."

"Be glad I do not demand more for my silence. I know you hid yourself in this hole and thought I wouldn't know where to find you, but you'll soon learn that you should have never left Cape Town, because you can never escape those who know the truth. Good-bye until I call again no matter where you might hide."

"You're not to call again!" he objected.

"We'll see. Just for the present I'm in no mood to quarrel with you, and you'd better not quarrel with me if you know what is good for you."

She tucked the check into her purse and ambled out of the room after a supercilious nod to Alice, who failed to respond in any manner. Her discombobulated father stood, still frowning, until Jane's high-heeled shoes had clattered down the stairs. Alice went to the window and looking down saw that a chauffeured Rolls Royce was at the curb. Jane entered the car and was whisked away.

There are times when we see but do not truly perceive. There are times when we hear but do not understand. There are times when we touch but do not feel. There are times when reality seems before us but the situation itself seems unreal. There are times when the clouds obscure the light of day so completely that we can sense no warmth from the sun, which we know is there despite it being covered by darkness. This was a time that dear Alice instinctively knew there was something sinister afoot, but she could not discern just what it was, and who might be involved. She longed to find answers, but knew not where to turn. For a moment she felt slight resentment toward her mother, having left her in such precarious circumstances. How she longed for the safety of her mother's arms.

Lynton and the Cape Town Ghost

Alice turned to look at her father. He was breathing heavily, as he eased into a chair. Then Alice looked over at the painting and a sense of foreboding overwhelmed her, as she could not believe what she saw. She felt chills run up her spine as she stood just staring in disbelief at the painting.

A painting is an absolutely remarkable thing in form and style, but what Alice saw was overpowering. When an artist puts brush to canvas there is a channelling of the soul into the images, and the images can have a potent emotional impact. One can be moved to tears, reduced to a depressed wreck, be elevated to marked inspiration, uplifted, disgusted or experience a whole spectrum of emotions by merely looking at paint on canvas. But this painting sent a chill through Alice like a cold, icy wind descending from a mountain of evil.

How had her father had time to draw what she saw? The lady in the veil had moved closer to the reclining lady by the stream with the vial now dripping a white liquid. The lady by the stream had outstretched hands pleading not to be forced to swallow the elixir.

Alice could not speak. She only looked at her father and pointed at the painting. Shock overwhelmed James Shriver as he looked at it. All he could do was stare in disbelief as he shouted, "I did not paint that."

Alice ran to her room in tears, as her father sat staring in perplexed dismay at the painting. He could not take his eyes from it. There was an intense fear that made his heart pound with furious intensity. Had Alice secretly painted what he was staring at in shock?

This was the first of many incidents that would plague Alice's young mind and cause James, when looking at a painting that seemed to be completing itself, to sometimes doubt his sanity.

Chapter 3
Icy Hand of Fate or the Warmth of Hope

Alice stood stoically beside a canvas on an easel one morning after nearly two years had passed, watching her father work. Not that she was especially interested in him or the painting, but there was nothing else to do. She stood with slim legs apart, intense look upon her face, hands clasped behind her back, staring vacantly, when James looked up and noted her presence.

"Well, what do you think of it?" he asked rather sharply.

Contemplating as she stared at the nearly two year old painting he had resurrected, noticing that he had painted over a part of the painting where a vial had been dripping a white substance, and the lady by the stream had lost a previous scowling look of fear and was now smiling, she said, "I liked it the way it was. It was scary then."

"You liked it that way 'cause you did that one."

Shocked at his accusation, she replied, "I did not touch your old painting; although, I could have drawn it better than you. My mother obviously had no idea just how horrible an artist you are."

He laid down his palette and brush and gazed at his painting for a long time. He was breathing heavily. His lips were contorted, puckering up and quivering. A menacing scowl came upon his face. Usually his face was stolid and expressionless, but Alice had begun to observe over the years that whenever anything irritated or disturbed him he scowled, and the measure of the scowl indicated to what extent he was annoyed. When he scowled at his own unfinished painting, Alice decided he was realizing just how untalented he was.

Finally, James reached beside his palette and took a knife from the table, opened the blade and deliberately slashed the picture from top to bottom, this way and that, until it was a mere mass of shreds. Then he kicked the destroyed painting into a corner and brought out another canvas, which he placed on the easel. He looked with anger at her, and said, "I'll start all over. That make your happy?"

Alice was frightened by his violent act and with quivering voice said, "It's your masterpiece. Do what you like with it. I could absolutely care less what you do."

"You'll care, because if I am displeased with my work I am an ogre."

Smiling, Alice, who could be curt when confronted with anger, replied, "Then you must be displeased all the time, because you have appeared to be an ogre for two years now."

James, knife still in his hand, walked over to a stack of his paintings and one by one slashed them to shreds. He tossed each one into the corner with the others, destroying the unsellable paintings. Shriver was not scowling any more. Instead, there was a somewhat satisfied expression on his usually dull features, as he destroyed each and every one of his paintings.

Alice was perplexed at the mad act, for although her judgment told her they were not worth keeping, she realized that her father must have passed many laborious hours on them. But now that it had dawned on him how utterly inartistic his work was, in humiliation and disgust, he had wiped all his work out of existence. It was then that a wave of pity overwhelmed Alice, as she genuinely felt sorry for the poor man.

Still, Shriver did not seem sorry for what he had done. When the last ruined canvas had been contemptuously flung into the corner, he turned to the child and said to her in a cheerful voice, "That was liberating, and thank you for your honesty. It hurt yes, but sometimes the truth does hurt. Get your hat and let's take a walk. An artist's studio is no place for us on a bright sunshiny day like this. Come, your father is liberated at last. From now on I shall always paint without concern for commercialization, but for pure artistic joy."

The rest of the day he behaved much like a normal human being. He took Alice to the park and bought her popcorn and peanuts, a wild extravagance for him. Later in the day they walked all about and finally entered an upscale restaurant, quite different from the one where they had often previously eaten and enjoyed a fine dinner and good humour. When they left the restaurant, he was still in a good mood and said, "Let's stroll about Piccadilly for awhile. Who wants to go back to that drab flat? Hey, what about the theatre? You like Shakespeare?"

"Of course."

Suppose we go to the Avalon Theatre? The Taming of the Shrew is playing."

"My favourite," responded Alice.

They had cheap balcony seats, first row overlooking the box seats below. Just before the curtain rose Alice noticed several parties being seated in the box seats. One of the ladies was dressed in an elaborate evening gown. It was Jane Arnold, and the man with her was none other than the attorney, Armand Hardy. What was he doing in London?

Alice glanced at her father's face and saw he had noticed them, for he had a look of recognition. However, neither of them made any remark and sat back to enjoy the play. But, on occasion, Alice would glance over at her father and notice that his eyes were not on the stage, but on the dark box seats below them, where Nurse Arnold and Mr. Hardy were sitting.

As they left the theatre, Arnold and Hardy were entering a chauffeured Rolls Royce, laughing and chatting gaily. Both father and daughter silently watched them depart, again, making no mention to one another of what they saw.

James, as they strolled home, was largely silent until he blurted out, "We are going to Cape Town."

"What," she replied.

"We are going back to Cape Town," he replied disappointedly. "Never should have left in the first place."

In absolute shock at the revelation, Alice now was silent herself. What would have possessed him to want to return to Cape Town? She was pleased, but could not help but wonder what could possibly have been the motivating factor. Was it the fact Arnold and Hardy had showed up?

Back once again in the drab flat, James barked for Alice to be off to bed, as he sat down and looked at his destroyed paintings over in the corner. Alice went to bed, exhilarated by the sudden humanity displayed by her father for a brief time, but perplexed now that he had reverted back to his usual sullen mood.

When she came out of her room next morning, she heard her father stirring in the studio. She went to him and was surprised to find him packing his trunk, which he had drawn into the middle of the room.

"Now that you're up," he said cheerfully "we'll go to breakfast, and then I'll help you pack your things. Only one trunk, though, for the other must go into storage and you may see it again, some time, or you may not."

He looked over at the painting on the easel, then back at her. She, too, looked at the painting and her jaw dropped, as she uttered, "Why did you paint that again?"

Looking at the easel with intent for the first time that morning, he stared in disbelief, as there was the woman lying by the stream again but with a look of fear on her face and another woman in the veil with a bottle dripping from it a white substance. James shouted, "You did that!"

"I did not!"

"You are playing your little tricks again. I see you are up to mischief. This will not do."

Almost pleading she replied, "I did nothing. You are the artist, not me."

Shaking his head, James retorted, "It doesn't matter. You can play your games back in Cape Town. We are off. Two years here is enough."

"Why? I am not complaining, because I prefer Cape Town to London, but why there?"

"Why not? It is the home of your mother's empire, and that empire will one day be yours, so why not take you back there?"

"That's the first thing you have done that makes me happy," she offered with a tinge of delight.

He laughed, and the laugh shocked her. She could not remember ever to have heard him genuinely laugh before. Through his grin, he said, "I don't like this place. That's why I'm leaving it. I was a fool to return here for appearances sake."

He looked at the painting, reached for his knife and cut it to shreds as he had done the others, but then he picked up a blank canvas, put it under his arm and said, "I'll take this along in case I get an inspiration, or in case you want to play your little sinister painting games."

She knew it would be futile to say again that it was not she who had done the previous paintings, because he was convinced she had some nefarious intent. Still, she wondered why he would do the paintings and then ascribe them to her.

Alice was eager to begin packing and hurried through her breakfast. All the things she might need on a journey she put into one trunk. She was not quite sure what she ought to take, but finally her trunk was packed and locked. Then James called a van taxi and carted away the extra trunks of Alice's and several boxes of his own to be deposited in a storage warehouse.

She sat in the bare studio and waited for his return. The monotony of the past two years, which had grown oppressive, was about to end and for this she was very grateful. From a life of luxury the child had been dumped into a gloomy studio in the heart of a big, bustling city that was all unknown to her and where she had not a single friend or acquaintance. Her only companion had been a strange man who happened to be her father but displayed no affection for her, no spark of interest in her happiness or even comforts, save that one brief time in the park and at the play. For the first time in her life she lacked a maid to dress her and keep her clothes in order; there was no one to attend to her education, no one to amuse her, no one to have counsel with as she dealt with her depression. She had been somewhat afraid of her peculiar father and her natural reserve, derived from her mother, had deepened. She realized there was a gulf between them that probably would never be bridged. Her father differed utterly from her mother in breeding, in intelligence, in sympathy. Yet, he was her father and all she had left to depend upon. She wondered if he really possessed the good qualities her mother had attributed to him. If so, she had not seen them, and why would he refuse to admit to painting that horrendous painting? Why did he insist that she drew it?

He was gone a long time, but as soon as he returned the remaining baggage was lugged down the stairs by the two of them with considerable strain. They were then unceremoniously loaded onto a waiting mini-van cab that apparently drove off to deliver them to whatever place they would board transportation for Cape Town and her father whispered directions to the driver as they headed down the street in a hurried manner. On lower Regent Avenue, they entered a bank, where she sat in the lobby while her father apparently transacted considerable business. Alice saw him receive several papers and a great deal of cash. Then they went to a cruise ship office near by, where her father purchased tickets. Why she wondered were they not flying to Cape Town?

Afterward, they had lunch and James was exhibiting high spirits and seemed to be eager and excited. He even became conversive.

"We're going by ship to Cape Town, because I think we both need relaxation. The sea air will be good for us, and we can enjoy our leisurely journey before we finally settle down and get you started in school. You are going to public school. There will be no tutors.

She had always been tutored, but she assumed the school would an exclusive private one, so it probably would not be bad, but his next words were shocking.

"You'll go to a normal public school and make some common friends, not the high-toned, arrogant children of the rich as has been your custom in the past. A daughter of mine will have the common touch, and you get that by mingling with the common people."

She was shocked, but also found herself curiously wondering what it would be like to go to a regular school, and as her father said, "mingle with the common people." Anyway, what choice did she have?

He seemed a somewhat, at least, emendable sort as he said during their hurried lunch, "so if there is anything you positively need for the trip, tell me what it is and I'll buy it. No frivolities, though," he said, qualifying his generosity, "but just necessities. And you must think quickly, for our boat leaves at four o'clock and we've no time to waste."

Alice shook her head. Once she had been taken by her mother to London, Marseilles and Rome, but all her wants had been attended to and it was so long ago that voyage was now but a dim remembrance in a poor mind that was dealing with the stark realities of just how much her life had changed since the death of her mother.

No one noticed them when they left. There was no one on the dock to see them off or to fondly wish them "bon voyage." It saddened poor, dear Alice to hear the fervent good-byes of the others there, for it emphasized her own intense loneliness, a loneliness that would grow as she watched her former life slowly fade into the oblivion of time.

She was stuck with a strange and incredibly uncongenial man whom fate had imposed upon her in the guise of a parent. As they steamed out to sea and Alice sat on deck and watched the receding shores of England, she turned to her father with the first question she had ventured to ask about the trip. "Why father? Why are you doing this?"

"I am a man with a past, a past that is catching up to me every day, Alice. I cannot stay in England, because my destiny awaits me in Cape Town, be it good, bad or indifferent. A reckoning will one day greet me with the icy hand of fate or the warmth of hope."

Chapter 4
Hell-Bent on Causing Havoc

Charlie Manson sang the song in his cell.
Then Marilyn Manson rang the alarm bell.
Asking if the world was really round,
Where the blue bird of happiness might be found.
We all want to know why the sky above is so blue.
When you were a child did anyone tell you?
What becomes of the sun when it falls to the sea?
And who lights it again as bright as it can be?
Why can no one fly without wings in the skies?
Why are there so many tears in people's eyes?

Charlie Manson sang the song in his cell.
Then Marilyn Manson rang the alarm bell.
Yes, yes, it is true the world is really round.

Lynton and the Cape Town Ghost

And the bluebird may one day be found.
And the sky up above may be crystal clear
So that you'll see the bluebird if it should appear.
And the sun doesn't fall when it slips out of sight.
All it does is make way for the moon's pretty light.
If we could fly, there would be no need for birds.
People cry, because they are touched by words.

Charlie Manson sang the song in his cell.
Then Marilyn Manson rang the alarm bell.
Don't be sad if it's true the world's round.
Search everywhere until the bluebird is found.
But there is no need to wander very far.
For what you really seek is where you are.
Show me some love and here is what I will do.
I will take the dear bluebird and give it to you.
Put the bluebird's love in your heart so true,
So heaven will shine its bright light on you.

Lynton Viñas was sipping rooibos tea as she sat on the veranda of the Labia Theatre on Orange Street in the Gardens District of Cape Town. She was with her friend Thatoo, but was still lonely because her husband, Wayne, had to go on another one of his dreaded Canadian and European book tours that seemed to always be keeping them apart. As was his custom, he had thoroughly admonished her before he left to not get involved in any adventures, because it seemed that when he was away, she was sought out by those who had turmoil in their lives, and ultimately that put her in a position of danger.

Lynton and the Cape Town Ghost

As her friend Thatoo excused himself for class at the International Hotel School, where they were both studying for advanced degrees, she waved goodbye and continued sipping her tea. It was a typical Cape Town day. A light breeze was blowing, the sun was shining and Lynton, always oblivious to the distractions she caused as a result of her beauty, was looking about the lovely place where she and her husband spent so many good times, not just watching European movies, but where they had made friends of all the staff and had embraced the quaint ambiance of an old-time movie house with four screens that had no place for trite entertainment from Hollywood where blowing things up, utilizing elaborate special effects and having people parade around naked passed for entertainment. This was not a movie theatre. It was a cinema!

You could look into her eyes and know that all the beauty of the universe could not even hope to compete with the simple exoticness that flashed in those dark orbs of passion. Passion, not of the flesh, but of the heart that turned her eyes into flames of raging fire, and in them one could read clearly that she would fight to the very last breath for justice in a world where it was in short supply. She would not let the world break her or those who turned to her for help when burdened by the evils that lurked in the dark corners of lost hope where the monsters of greed, avarice, pride, envy and wrath were given free reign in a world that had long ago lost its way.

Lynton and the Cape Town Ghost

She had a kind of understated beauty; perhaps it was because she was so disarmingly uncaring about her attractiveness. In her native Philippines, she had been encouraged to enter beauty contests, but laughed them off to be demeaning and degrading as nothing more than sexual objectification of females. Her soft, supple brown skin was flawless. She exuded simplicity, making things easy, helping those around her to relax and be happy with what they had. Perhaps that is why her skin so radiantly glowed, as it was her inner beauty that lit her eyes and softened her features. When she smiled and laughed you couldn't help but smile along with her, even if it was just on the inside. To be in her company was to feel that you were basking in the warm rays of the sunshine that emanated from her soul.

She was an adult, but retained the intense exuberance of youth. She had that movie star look, not overly tall and willowy, but more like an action star with taunt muscles. Her waist length black hair fluttered about as she rose and walked with confident strides off the veranda toward the sidewalk. Her wiggle could make a man get sea sick as her hips swayed side to side like a sleek yacht bounding over undulating waves. This was absolute perfection in a woman.

A short distance down the street, Alice Shrier was just walking into her father's artist studio, a loft off the living room. She gazed at a partially finished painting of a woman lying by stream as another woman in a veil was approaching.

Lynton and the Cape Town Ghost

Alice Shriver could not understand why her father kept drawing that same painting. Was he going crazy? They had been back in Cape Town only two days, and there it was again. Then, she looked out of the corner of her right eye and saw something that sent shivers up and down her spine. Standing in the doorway to the loft was a woman, a beautiful woman, despite her face being covered by a veil. In an almost transparent sheer negligee, this woman beckoned her with both hands, motioning for Alice to come toward her. Alice could not move, and in the blink of an eye, her father walked in through the doorway.

Her father shouted, "You are at it again aren't you?"

Ignoring the question, Alice could only incoherently mutter, "Didn't you see the lady?"

"Lady? All I see is you standing there painting again. Why do you persist in doing this?"

Still in shock at what she had seen, Alice, in an almost whisper, said, "I have told you. I have never painted anything. I am tired of the accusations."

Her emotions were on edge. She rushed by her father through to the living room and out the door. As she pounded on the elevator button her fury rose, and she whispered to herself through tears, "Why mamma did you do this? Why did you leave me in such dire circumstances? Where am I to go? What am I to do? I wish I was dead like you. Only in death will I ever find any peace. Only the darkness of the grave can console my pain."

Lynton and the Cape Town Ghost

Walking at a brisk pace down Orange Street, Alice noticed a shady spot by the University of Cape Town campus, a nice little niche by the Drama Department building. She followed a well worn path to the edge of the building and then walked through a small gate into Company's Gardens Park, which was a favourite place for Lynton to stroll through as she went to classes, and although she had no classes on this day, she was enjoying her leisurely walk through the park.

Lynton walked past the gate that opened into the Hiddighah campus of the University of Cape Town. She noticed the young girl with a look of deep consternation on her face. The girl walked through the ornamental gate and turned to walk down the brick pathway. Always aware of people who seemed to be dealing with turmoil and pain, Lynton just casually said, "hello," as a gesture of kindness.

With a look of shock, Alice replied, "Hi." She then, as the two walked side-by-side, continued, "I know you. I would recognize you anywhere. I have read all of Wayne Frye's Lynton books. You are the famous demon fighter."

"I am trying to give that up at the insistence of my husband, who does not take kindly to me always seemingly getting involved in mysteries that often defy explanation. I am now a student here, and I have hopefully left all that behind me."

"Oh my, I hate to impose on you then, but it is rather propitious that I have run into you just when I am faced with a ghost-like dilemma."

Lynton and the Cape Town Ghost

Lynton knew she should simply ignore what the young girl said and walk away, but that eternal spark within her that lights the flame of curiosity simply would not let her do it. As she began to open her mouth, while the words were coming out she was thinking, "Wayne's gonna be angry with me."

Still, despite her trepidation, she said, "And why is meeting me so propitious?"

"You won't believe it, but just this morning I think I saw a ghost, and, in reality, that was not the first time; although, this time was the most obvious."

Lynton pointed to a nearby bench, and the two took a seat. The sun was gradually disappearing, as dark clouds slowly crept in front of it. The shadows of darkness bounced about Alice's poor painful expression that seemed to make her appear far older than her tender years. Lynton, as the bright sunshine faded into darkness when clouds covered the sun, could not help but remember a poem her husband shared with her long ago.

I have been one acquainted with the night.
I have strolled out in warmth and back in cold.
I have out walked the furthest city light.

I have looked down the saddest town lane.
I have passed by the watchman on his beat
And dropped my eyes, unable to explain.

I have stood still and heard ghostly feet,

Lynton and the Cape Town Ghost

When far away an interrupted cry
Came over houses from another street.

Is it a ghost come to say a final goodbye?
Oh, the darkness surrounds me now
As if it is one luminary clock against the sky.

Proclaimed the time was neither wrong nor right,
I can smell the embers of death burning about.
I am someone slowly being shielded from light.

Lynton, gentle soul of understanding, placed her left hand on Alice's right shoulder, patting it with affection as she said, "Be not afraid my dear. I am willing to listen to all who carry heavy burdens in a world that offers little solace or compassion. I am but a lone voice of concern who often shouts in the wilderness of lost hope, and unfortunately there are few who heed the call to uplift those burdened with despair. I am called a demon hunter, a ghost buster, a vampire destroyer and more often, a nosy blunderer who should mind her own business. I am probably more the later. I simply cannot help but have my interest piqued when the words ghost, ghoul, vampire or poltergeist are bandied about. As I have said, my husband is never pleased with my penchant for adventure, because, as a result of his deep and abiding love, it causes him great consternation. In fact, he says he never had a headache in his entire life until he met me, and now I am his little headache."

Lynton and the Cape Town Ghost

As intended, the little homily put a smile on Alice's face. She said with great affection, "You are well-known for your humanity and commitment to justice for the downtrodden. Thank you for your willingness to listen to me."

"Listening is what I do best. So tell me Alice Shriver, what can I do for you?"

Shocked that she knew her name, Alice asked, "How to you know me?"

"Remember that my husband is also the author of the Aaron Adams novels, and Aaron is the greatest detective since Phillip Marlow, Sam Spade and Mike Hammer," she said with a knowing smile as she looked down at the bag Alice was carrying. "My husband; therefore, has taught me some of the tricks of the private detective trade."

"But how?"

Interrupting her, Lynton continued, "The locket around your neck my dear girl has an "A" engraved on it. Just a logical deduction on my part that your name might be Alice, since I also glanced at the very expensive phone you have in your hand that simply flashed your last name as you were fidgeting with it as you sat down. You, based upon your clothes, the Gucci bag and the aforementioned expensive phone, are from a wealthy background, and I know of the Shriver Cosmetics firm, and of the young daughter named Alice whose mother, Ann Shriver, died a while back. Elementary, my dear, elementary, as Sherlock Holmes would say!"

Lynton and the Cape Town Ghost

Smiling a bit through her serious demeanour, Alice's eyes were beaming with admiration, knowing that she had just met a remarkable woman, as she said, "Wow!"

Lynton, again gently placing her left hand on Alice's right shoulder, said, "Not wow actually, just deductive reasoning based upon my penchant for reading several daily newspapers on-line and knowing the history of your mother. Now, tell me more about this apparition that you have apparently seen."

"You will listen, then?"

Getting up and motioning for Alice to do the same, Lynton said, "Sure, let us stroll about the park as you tell me about what you have experienced. Walking is good when you are overwhelmed with worries, even on a dark day like this one."

So they turned off the paved walkway onto a little path, not talking, as Lynton wanted to let things flow naturally without prodding. They presently came upon a labourer who was very deliberately but methodically cultivating the plants along the path with a V-shaped hoe. Seeing the strangers, the man straightened up and eyed them with evident suspicion. "Good afternoon," said the old black gentleman in the Xhosa language that a mere generation ago he had been forced to not use as the apartheid government insisted everyone speak either Afrikaans or English. He loved using it around white people which Alice was, simply as a form of independence.

Lynton and the Cape Town Ghost

To his complete shock, Lynton, who speaks eight languages fluently and has a working knowledge of several others, replied in Xhosa, "Kwaye mhle mva kuwe (good afternoon to you, too)."

Shocked that a Filipino would have mastered Xhosa, he continued conversing with her in his native language, but Lynton, ever cognizant of politeness, said, "Perhaps we should converse in English, so as not to exclude this young lady from understanding what we are saying."

"Oh, I speak English, of course," replied the man, doffing his hat. "I am Lungelo Labersham, and you must know that I can tell you are Filipino. When I worked in Dubai, I knew many Filipinos. Hard workers you are."

"Yes, we are, and I have had many relatives and friends who worked in Dubai. Like my countrymen and women, I guess you went there for the nice paycheques."

"Ah, I did indeed."

Looking up at Alice, who at her young age, was already considerably taller than the 5:2 Lynton, the dynamic dynamo of ghost hunting realized that she had interrupted the young girl's desire to unburden herself of the misery that had befallen her. She turned to the gardening man and said, "Nice talking with you, but we must be moving on now."

Alice's eyes danced hopefully as the two walked away toward the statue of Cecil John Rhodes. Alice whispered, "Thank you for listening."

"I have not listened much yet. So, please tell me about your ghostly experiences."

"Yes, being so astute, you indicated that you know of my mother's death."

"Of course."

Sighing, Alice said, "There was one strange occurrence an hour or so after mother's death, but later the apparitions began in earnest. I have seen apparitions several times, but have only mentioned it once to my father. It was this morning when I saw it clearer than ever before. He, however, said he did not see it. I am not sure whether he did see it or not. He could be lying."

Lynton observed her closely and interjected, "I have found it not uncommon for some people to see apparitions when others cannot. It is rumoured that it is because some of us are more psychically attuned than others. Myself, I am not sure I have ever seen an apparition, and I am not even sure I believe in them, but nonetheless, I am open minded, and just because I am not sure about them does not mean they do not exist. Continue please."

"First, you must be aware that watching my mother die was a horrific experience. I observed her slowly fade into oblivion, and it seemed to me that everyone around her was cold and aloof about her impending death. It was at this time I began to think that I must slip into her room to sit by her side and hold her hand, letting her know that I was there for her, that I loved her, that I needed for her to stay with me, not leave me alone in a world that seems overwhelming at times. This I did on a regular basis while the nurse slept or while she was temporarily away. It seemed everyone wanted to keep me from my mother."

They turned to their left and walked past the planetarium to the Gardens Café, where they sat down to order scones and tea. Alice, a look of consternation upon her young face, displayed all the anguish that had been piling up for so long. Finally, she was unburdening herself, and she felt that Lynton genuinely cared.

"I have never given any credence to ghosts, but as I sat in that room after my mother's death, I felt a presence. There seemed to be something there that would make the hairs on the back of my neck prick up. I saw nothing, but I felt something was there, near my side. The feeling that something was in that room with me was overwhelming. I stood, walked to the door, turned and looked back at the bed. There seemed to be a faint glowing light hovering above my dear mother's bed. I did not shout with fear, but I was absolutely terribly chilled to the bone at first, but then a serene calmness came over me, and I looked at that hovering bluish light and it gradually changed hues. It hovered about for awhile and then dissipated."

"I rushed to the bedside, and looked down at where my dear beloved mother had lain on her bed. I had watched her so often having difficulty breathing, inhaling and exhaling with so much pain and so much discomfort. There was never any peacefulness about her toward the end, and at that moment, I felt serenity abide in me for a brief time. I left the room feeling that all might be well with me."

Lynton interjected, ""And you think that this apparition was good or bad?"

"I do not know!"

"So, this was your first encounter with the supernatural, but there have been others, no doubt."

"Oh, many more I am afraid. But what do you think of my first experience?"

"I do not have an opinion, but I have some suppositions. Yet, it is too early to explore them. Go on about the next time."

"Well, you have to know that I have never been very social, so I was alone most of the time with my governess. She is not a pleasant sort, and frankly I have grown over the years to despise her and was not unhappy when my father dismissed her. I wanted to share what I had seen with her, but she was disinterested in anything about me or my mother. All she cared about was assigning my lessons, grading them and then doing her infernal reading while ignoring me. After the arrival of my father, he basically ignored me, seemed disinterested in my welfare, and one day as he was away in the separate room he had taken in the hotel I sat merely staring out the window while my governess slept. It was a cloudy day and the grey skies made the room exceedingly dark. I was so tired that I drifted off asleep, too. I was presently awakened, though."

Lynton and the Cape Town Ghost

Lynton, as she buttered her scone, said, "And some presence in the room awakened you."

Letting out a faint smile, Alice replied, "You are very good. One could get the impression you anticipate what comes next."

"Years of experience, my dear Alice, have made me anticipatory when I comes to ghosts."

"I saw nothing that time, only felt something. It was a hand, a hand with thin, long fingers I would say that touched me from the rear of the sofa on the shoulder. Yet, when I turned, no one was there."

"Did the hand feel warm or cold?" asked Lynton.

"I am not sure, as I was too shocked and frightened to notice."

"Go on."

"I found myself strangely drawn to my mother's room, the room where she died. It was almost as if a sinister force was pulling me there. I would often sit there for hours by the bed. I would find myself reaching over to the bed as if she were still there, wanting to hold her hand, which I did on so many occasions when she was ill."

Alice's face grew sterner, as she continued. "Out of the window to my right I could see the garden by the waterfront with those mysterious deep-shaded arbours, the riotous old-fashioned flowers, bushes and gnarly trees that seemed to take on sinister shapes, mimicking goblins. Beyond the garden was a lovely view of the bay and a little private wharf where my mother kept our sail boat, which we had not used for many months due to her illness. There is a beautiful shaded lane that runs down there from the hotel. I would sit by the bed and imagine walking down there with my mother, walking together and laughing as we so often had. I was reminiscing about all the good times, grasping nostalgia like it was a long lost friend that somehow was waiting for me, waiting to wrap me in its warmth."

Alice sighed and then paused. It was obvious to Lynton that she was now drifting back into a time when all was right with the world, a time when she knew the glory of being loved, a time when she felt safe. Lynton leaned forward and said, "You will always have those memories. As time passes, the memories will not die, but you will find new memories to savour. Go on now dear, and tell me of what occurred. What made you think you were seeing a ghost that time?"

"I noticed the wallpaper in the room was beginning to tear, starting from the corner of the room opposite from where I was sitting. There was something about that wallpaper. There was no reason for it to be peeling. It was obviously relatively new. The wallpaper pattern began to interest me. No, it seemed to be whispering to me. The wallpaper had a kind of sub-pattern in a different shade, a particularly irritating one, for you can only see it in certain lights, and not clearly then. But in the places where it wasn't faded by the sunlight that beat upon it, I could see a strange, provoking, formless sort of figure that appeared to sulk about behind what seemed an exceedingly silly and conspicuous front design. I heard a moan, a faint moan from behind the wall I supposed. I could not tell whether the voice was male or female, as it was hoarse, so hoarse and low that I had to strain my ears to comprehend the slow agonizing moan. Then I heard it, heard it whispering so very low a warning. It mumbled simply two words – *be vigilant.* I blinked my eyes, looked with intensity at the wall paper, but there was no further sound. I heard the wooden floor squeak by the bed and then felt that same long, soft finger touch my hand. There was no one there, of course, only the feel of that hand, which was gone within a split second."

"From that day forward I was determined to not be afraid, but rather, to go into that room each day and see if something was there, something that was trying to communicate with me. I actually found myself sometimes lying on the bed in the very spot where my mother had died. I would spend hours just staring at the wallpaper, staring continuously in the hope I would hear that voice again, hear it say something that might lift me from my pit of despair. I would follow the patterns on the wallpaper, and I determined I would follow the seemingly pointless patterns to some sort of a conclusion. I asked myself if the wallpaper itself was trying to communicate with me. I know a little of the principle of design, and I know the wallpaper was not arranged on any laws of design or repetition, or symmetry or anything else."

Lynton and the Cape Town Ghost

Alice's voice trembled. "I know this sounds crazy to you, but I am telling you I felt there was something behind that wallpaper."

Lynton was amazed at how articulate a girl this young was. Her use of language was descriptive, cogent and colourful.

Alice continued. "There seemed to be an optic horror to what I was seeing in that wallpaper. No, not horror, wait, it was more like a beckoning; a call for me to somehow join whatever it was in that wall. All the figures in it were causing a swirl in my brain. They connected diagonally, and the sprawling outlines ran off in great slanting waves of a sort of optic horror, like a lot of wallowing seaweeds inundating on the ocean surface. The pattern also went horizontally, too, at least it seemed so, and I exhausted myself in trying to distinguish the order of its going in all directions. The cross-light in the room faded and the low sun shined directly upon the patterns. There the paper seemed to radiate as an interminable form took shape around a common centre. It was more shadow than anything else, and it was more grey than black. I could not move, as I was frozen on that bed, and then the moan came again, low, gravelly, strained and almost pleading. The shape was taking on a form, but it was still too faint to make out whether it was male or female, but I discerned that it must be female. Oh, and that moan became more a plea, a plea for assistance. I knew whatever it was had great pain, a longing for someone to comprehend its agony."

Lynton and the Cape Town Ghost

Lynton could tell that recounting the episode was causing great angst, but she dare not interrupt her, because she felt that the only way to help the poor girl was to hear her out. Lynton was now fascinated and intrigued not only by the tale of foreboding woe, but by the eloquently fluent way in which she was describing it.

Pausing to take a sip of her tea and a bite of the scone, Alice eagerly continued. "I never shared this with anyone, because I thought they might think me crazy, and I feared that my uncaring father might actually have me dispatched to an asylum. You see, I got so addicted to that room, to my mom's death bed that I would lie in it every chance I would get, whether it be day or night. But, of course, only when I knew that I would not be discovered. Sometimes the patterns on the wallpaper seemed to jump out at me, and other times, at night, when the moon was out, that grey shadow would creep out of the wall slowly, and almost appear to dance about, but never was it able to completely get out of that wallpaper. It was maybe three-fourths out and one-fourth in. I had not the courage to arise and confront it face-to-face. Oh, but always that wail would come, the pleading and then there was also moaning, moaning that seemed to come from deep within the thing's soul. I often found myself crying with sympathy for the poor creature, the thing that was obviously reaching out to me, trying to somehow seek solace from someone in a world of which it was no longer a part."

Lynton and the Cape Town Ghost

"I tried to stay out of the room, because I was becoming physically sick and mentally distraught. Alas, after two days I had to return. It was as if something was calling me. I could not fight the urge to be there. It was no longer about being in the room where my mother died to somehow feel nearer her. Rather, it was the need now to help this thing, whatever it was. My empathy for it still did not assuage my fear of it though, because I felt that it might have sinister intentions. I would lie there on the bed early in the evening as the moon's rays shot in through the east window by the bay. I always watched for that first long, straight ray that would almost seem like a beacon luring whatever was in that wall out of its hibernation. Then, as the moon shone in one night when it was full, the grey figure seemed to almost make it out of the wall, only a hand remaining within. Oh, but then I could see something not seen before. This grey shadow seemed to darken, and I could make out its clothing. It was a long flowing nightgown. Yes, for sure, it was a woman!"

"Oh, and the moaning became more intense. Yet, I could not rise from the bed and confront it. I was too afraid. Suddenly, it dissipated."

"Then one day when I decided to creep into the room as it was around noon-time, I slowly pushed the door inward and there was the shock of my life. I could not believe it. My father was there and he was stroking the wallpaper, as if searching for something. The shock of seeing me made him stop, as he turned and asked why I was there."

Lynton and the Cape Town Ghost

"I avoided the question and asked him, with the most restrained manner possible, why he was in the room. He stared intensely as if he had been caught stealing something, and he looked quite angrily at me. He shouted as he walked past me out of the room that I should mind my own business and stay out of that infernal room."

Lynton leaned slightly forward, saying, "Do you think he was seeing the apparition, too?"

"I am not sure. However, I actually think not perhaps. He knew something unusual was happening though, and I believe that was a motivating factor in his ultimate decision to leave Cape Town. Several weeks later he announced our imminent departure."

Her interest piqued now, Lynton said, "But you kept going into the room. You were drawn to it?"

"Oh yes dear Lynton, definitely yes. But there was something else about that paper. It was developing a foul smell. I noticed it the moment I came in the room the day after the incident with my father. I was disturbed by the smell, as it was faint at first, but very slowly it began to permeate the room. Oh, it smelled as if something was decaying. The only way to describe the smell is to equate it to what I once read in the book *Something Evil in the Darkness at Hopkins House* by your husband. I am sure you have read it. Aaron Adams, his detective is in the evil room where an entity is floating about, wrecking havoc on Aaron's psyche and it was not just the ghost he feared, but it was the smell, the infernal smell."

Lynton and the Cape Town Ghost

Lynton took a deep breath and sighed, as she said, "Oh yes, I have read it, and it is my favourite of all his books. The smell was not of this earth he proclaimed. It was a smell from the bowels of the earth, where rotting corpses burned in purgatory trying to free themselves to move on to either a lower or higher plain. It was the smell of painful, agonizing misery of not the physical but of the soul. It was the smell of souls crying out for mercy where there was none, souls that could not escape from the torment that bound them in perpetual, agonizing, unrelenting pain of the spirit."

"Yes, that is it exactly, and I always wept, because I could tell this ghost or whatever it was did not want to haunt me to create fear or any evil, but to somehow appeal to me to in some way help. Yet, it was unable to communicate its desires. There was some barrier that kept it from ever speaking, but just that one time."

"But it did not stay in that wall did it?" asked Lynton.

"No, it started creeping all over the house as sort of a mist or dark shadow. I saw it hovering in the dining-room, skulking in the parlour, hiding in the hall, lying in wait for me on the stairs, often not in any discernable form, but just in a feeling that somehow it was there but not seen, and I believe it also did something very unusual to unnerve both me and my father. It was apparently able to toy with a canvas on an easel, a painting that could never be finished, as it was started over and over again."

Lynton and the Cape Town Ghost

Intensely interested, Lynton said, "And the smell continued, too?"

"Yes, definitely, and I would ask my father about it and he would say that he smelled nothing, but I suspect he did. Again, I believe that is why he eventually decided to leave, believing that once out of those rooms and away from that damnable wall paper that we would both be free of this thing, but never once did he say anything of it, anything to indicate he could smell that horrible odour or see the shadows."

"And you see this thing or sense it or smell it at all times of the day?"

"Yes. You know, at night sometimes I would be in that room and there would be no indication it was there. Then very late in the evening, after midnight, I would sometimes look out the window and in the reflection behind me I could see its undulating form taking shape. I was no longer fearful, but rather fascinated. I felt it would do me no harm. Yet, when I would turn, it was gone. Then I would look in the window again. There it was undulating behind me. Once, just out of curiosity of what it might do, I did not turn. Rather, I simply kept staring into the window. It moved slowly toward me, but not in a menacing way. It reached out and touched my shoulder with what was an icy, bone chilling hand so cold that I actually believed I might turn to a block of ice from the touch. I knew if I turned that it would dissipate immediately, so I just stood there mesmerized, not moving."

Lynton and the Cape Town Ghost

Lynton interjected, "And it, no doubt, was unable to communicate, so you turned in hopes that it might be able to, but again it just disappeared."

"Yes, you are perceptive. How do you know so many things about this type of occurrence?"

"I have had much experience with the supernatural my dear Alice. There is a pattern to most of these apparition manifestations."

"Is it possible Lynton for a ghost to haunt more than one place?"

"There are incidents where a ghost haunts a person rather than a place. I am always a sceptic, but I do know cases where people have left houses they thought haunted only to have those ghosts follow them. Now, in my estimation that might well be simply people's minds playing tricks on them, but I discount nothing as fact or fiction. There simply are things in life which are truly unexplainable. And, of course, this ghost followed you to London, and now back to Cape Town, where it first manifested itself to you. Am I right?"

"Yes."

"You need tell me no more of the manifestations at this point. As Sherlock Holmes used to tell Dr. Watson, '*the game is afoot*.' Let us go now Alice, so that I might meet your father, and attempt to tackle the dark forces that are apparently hell-bent on causing havoc."

Chapter 5
What of the Apparitions?

The spine tingles and the bones grow weak.
Chills come at every minor creak.
Even the faintest noise makes the heart jump.
Faster and faster it begins to pump.

There is initially the feeling of fear.
It makes reality become quite unclear.
They say the only thing to fear is fear itself,
But then a book untouched flies off the shelf.

There is the feeling of no longer being alone.
From somewhere there comes a dreadful moan.
Quite unsettling this eerie feeling can be,
When something seems to moan a plea.

Lynton and the Cape Town Ghost

Mysterious feelings like a shot in the dark
Sear through the pounding heart.
In the darkness you scramble for any light,
Fearful of the oncoming plight.

Figuring out what's real and what's imagination
Causes a flittering frustration.
There in the darkness fear lingers.
Then on the shoulder are felt icy fingers.

The room races round and round,
And suddenly quiet is found.
There is now some emotional control.
Something is penetrating the soul.

Suddenly an inner calm prevails.
What does this thing want as it wails?
Not feared but pitied now,
It has no intentions that are foul.

As they approached the house that Alice's father had rented, which was off Kloof Street in Cape Town's Gardens District, Alice sighed and said, "My father's passion is art. He knows nothing else. Always there is an easel and canvas before him. He does not often speak, especially to me; he does not have friends who visit him. He knows people, mostly in London obviously, but they show no like of him, no inclination toward friendship. I have no friends either, never have, as even my mother was a bit of a recluse, but very well liked by all who were acquainted with her."

Lynton and the Cape Town Ghost

"Sometimes friends are overrated, Alice. If you can count genuine friends in a lifetime on one hand you are fortunate. Friend is an over used word. Most people we know are mere acquaintances, not friends. There is a big difference."

"I so desperately need a friend right now, Lynton. I am so scared," offered Alice.

"Never be scared, Alice. Fear is what can keep people from standing against tyranny, whether it is the tyranny of the unexplained or the far too often explained. The world is full of self-serving, arrogant, narcissistic jerks that want to break the wings of those who stand against evil. I have battled the natural inclinations of evil practiced by the living, who are far more frightening than the non-living. I do not wallow in misery, nor do I fret. I am a woman who can keep flying, because I have a broomstick and an iron will like a witch on a midnight prowl. You don't mess with Lynton Viñas, and she is about to become your champion and real friend. Let's do some ghost busting."

The house was off the main thoroughfare, Camp Street, on a quaint tree-lined cul-de-sac where the imposing hilltop mansion sat elevated above the old Dutch inspired homes below. There, within the dreary looking residence of Alice and James Shriver, something was waiting.

There are surroundings that seem an ominous conduit for the supernatural. The rented mansion appeared to be a perfect match for father and daughter who both lived under a dark cloud. The house, seeming to pulsate with fear, stood by itself against the backdrop of famed, mercurial Table Mountain, whose crest was covered by fluffy hanging clouds, holding darkness within. The stucco walls of the house were darkened to dirt brown from years of neglect. The windows were caked in grime and for the most part shuttered, leaving only the slimmest of slithers for light to struggle through.

Alice opened the gate and the two cautiously walked along the stone steps toward the house, their ankles tickled by the tendrils of weeds that had broken through the cobbles. From only one window was there any light, while through the slanted shutters all the other rooms appeared to be drearily dark. The one light was different, like a lighthouse amber blinking a beacon of danger. Alice raised her dainty hand and gently held down the front door latch. It rattled a bit and then lurched open.

The entrance hall was expansive, airy and eerie. An uneasy breeze blew down the corridor and grasped the two with a chilly touch. Invisible fingers circled around their bodies, seeming to ominously embrace them. The door down the hallway to their right had been left ajar, allowing a dark shadow to pierce out from the doorway to meander and babble like a narrow stream winding through a crevice. Their minds told them not to move, but they were inexplicably pulled toward the shadow, as from within that room came a low, mournful whine. The notorious Cape Town wind was now howling outside like the tormented cries of a tortured person, blending with the whining of whatever it was in that room.

Suddenly, from atop the stairs, slowly walking down, James Shriver moved gingerly toward them as the shadow dissipated, as if frightened by his presence. Reaching the bottom of the stairs, very cautiously and curtly he blurted out, "And who is this?"

"This," replied Alice "is the famous demon hunter, Lynton Viñas."

"What's she doing here?"

"Father, I am concerned about things, unusual things I have been experiencing. Things I think you may have experienced, too, but kept to yourself. I thought she might help."

"Nonsense!"

"Pardon my intrusion," said Lynton, taking a deep breath, "I met your very extraordinary daughter in the park, and she simply shared some unusual stories about strange occurrences that genuinely interested me."

Shrugging his shoulders, James turned to his right and headed down the hallway. He murmured as he left, "Stay and do what you will, because I can see you are the kind of busybody that would go to the authorities if I threw you out, as I probably should. People like you are a nuisance. Just don't get in my way."

Alice led the perplexed Lynton into the room from whence the shadow and moans had come. She called for the maid to fetch tea and biscuits.

"As you can see, my father is not the hospitable sort," Alice sheepishly offered.

Lynton said, "There may be reasons for your father's curtness."

"Sometimes I feel that I shall go mad here, or anywhere, because this shadowy figure with its sorrowful moans seems intent on following me wherever we go. I am of no sound mind any longer I am afraid."

Smiling, Lynton replied, "You are of very sound mind, Alice. You prove it by the way you are approaching this whole affair. You are amazing for someone so young."

Lynton could feel Alice's silent cry for help. "I suppose," remarked the astute student of human behaviour, "that your father is so immersed in his own world of misery that he forgets his daughter needs the warmth of parental affection."

"My father dislikes society. I believe he would be quite content to live in this little cooped-up place forever and see no one but the servants, to whom he seldom speaks. Also, he ignores me, and I am glad he does. But before my mother died," her voice breaking a little, "I was greatly loved and petted, and I can't get used to the change. I ought not to say this to a stranger, I know, but I am very lonely and unhappy, because my father is so different from the way my mother was."

Lynton, sitting on the sofa beside Alice, reached over and holding her trembling hand while stroking it sympathetically, said, "Tell me more about your mother."

Lynton and the Cape Town Ghost

"I was her constant companion and she taught me to love art, for art was her hobby. I did not know my father in those days, you see, for they did not live together. But in her last illness mamma sent for him and made him my guardian. My mother said my father would love me, but she misjudged him. He seems incapable of loving anyone, including himself. Oh, how I wish I had a friend to console me, to understand the dark cloud that hangs over me."

"You have a friend," uttered Lynton, pressing the girl's hand, "and isn't it unusual we have met in this singular manner in a country where I thought I would escape my past of involvement in so many mysteries and adventures."

Lynton was thinking how much grief her husband would give her for once again getting involved in something that might cause him worry. He always affectionately referred to her as his little headache. Thinking of him made her smile as she said, "I gather your mother was mistaken about your father's artistic abilities?"

"She was," answered Alice with emphatic emphasis. "He is a disaster with canvas, brush and paint. An elementary school child has more talent than he. I have even observed him destroy most of his work. Really, it was dreadful! And since the day he took knife to canvas, I have seen him dabble, but never seriously try to paint. I think perhaps he has realized how talentless he is. Yet, there is a painting he seems to keep drawing, one of two women, one with a vial in her hand and another seemingly sickly lying in desperation. He claims it is I who is painting it, but it is not."

"Strange," offered Lynton, "I remember seeing a painting by a James Shriver I believe once in London, near Piccadilly. It was a landscape and seemed well executed, and that was the opinion of an art connoisseur with whom I was visiting the gallery."

"I am no art critic, but believe me; I have seen no talent exhibited by him. I value my mother's opinion on everything, but I sincerely believe she was blinded by love when it came to assessing my father's talent. I have also read somewhere that discouragement sometimes destroys one's talent, though in after years, with proper impulse, it may return with added strength. In my father's case, he was not able to sell his work anywhere from what I have seen and no wonder. So now I believe he justifiably, in my opinion, sees himself as an abject failure."

Amazed at the intelligence displayed by Alice, Lynton said, "And what of your schooling? Has it continued with tutors?"

"Are you kidding, Lynton? I am my own teacher now. I have no tutor. It is deplorable that he will not even allow me to attend any kind of school. What kind of father would do that to a daughter my age?"

Lynton hung her head, digesting what the poor girl had said, and she did not reply. What could she say in reply to such an abrogation of parental duty?

Lynton and the Cape Town Ghost

"None of this is any of your business little miss busy body," boomed James Shriver, who was standing in the doorway.

Lynton looked up at him as he sauntered into the room and took a seat. "I am not here to cause problems, Mr. Shriver. I just met Alice and was captivated by her tales of strange apparitions. I do have a great deal of experience in dealing with the supernatural. In fact, I have some of that experience right here in South Africa."

"I have heard of you. Anybody who reads the newspaper or watches CNN International would know of your exploits. All a bunch of hooey as far as I am concerned."

"Much of it," replied a smiling Lynton, "is definitely a lot of hooey. I am afraid embellishment is often practiced for effect."

He nodded, sitting now with his legs crossed, regarding his visitor with unconcealed suspicion. "Why would you be interested in what my daughter is obviously imagining?"

"Perhaps that is my fatal flaw, Mr. Shriver. A mystery of almost any kind always intrigues me."

"Nothing mysterious here. My daughter is simply imagining things."

Lynton slowly and steadily rose, just as the maid entered with the tea and biscuits. She looked down directly into Shriver's cold steel blue eyes. "I will go then. I have no right to explore the happenings without your approval. Your daughter is but a minor. If you want me gone, I have no choice but to leave."

Lynton and the Cape Town Ghost

Poor Alice looked over at her dad, pleading. "Please! Please father. I beg of you to not deny me this one favour. If she is not allowed to explore the strange things I have seen, I shall be as unruly as you could ever imagine, and I may well consider going to the police."

Hearing the word police seemed to send a shiver through his entire body. He appeared to be physically ill. He was breathing deeply and glaring first at Alice, then at Lynton, who still stood before him. "Sit down, woman," said James Shriver in a much less aggressive tone than the one he had employed previously. "I've no objection to your explorations, under certain parameters. Make yourself at home, I suppose. However, you will find my daughter simply producing things in her overly imaginative mind that is still reeling from her mother's death."

"Mr. Shriver, your daughter is an exceptionally bright girl, which, no doubt, reflects well on the genes she got from you and her mother."

Still, Shriver remained glum and was obviously harbouring indignation over his evidently forced acceptance of the fact Lynton would be poking her nose around the mansion. For some unknown reason, he was willing to bear the presence of the woman known as the dynamic dynamo.

Alice, in her father's presence, lost her fluent speech and no longer dared mention personal matters to Lynton, as she was fearful of her father's reaction. Lynton observed her reluctance and did not pursue the ghostly matters.

Lynton and the Cape Town Ghost

Lynton, realizing that only by getting her away from her father could she explore details of the ghostly apparitions further, said, "May I have the pleasure of your daughter's company on occasion? There are many things I enjoy in Cape Town, and having a young companion would make exploration more pleasurable."

"No," replied Shriver.

"Oh, why not, father?" pleaded Alice.

"You've got no business being away from home. This is where you belong."

"It will be a nice change for your daughter and it will give me much pleasure to entertain her. Perhaps we can talk of the things she has seen in an environment free of the shadows of darkness that seem to prevail here," said Lynton.

Shriver dropped his eyes, frowning, as deep furrows creased his brow. After a few seconds in thought, he resigned himself to the inevitable. "Go, if you want, but stay out of the Cape Town Flats area."

"Why?" asked his daughter in a defiant tone.

"It's just not a good area for you to be wandering around. I know the Flats, and the rascally ruffians around there would be glad to kidnap you, if they had the chance and then ransom you."

Laughing, Alice exclaimed, "What a grand adventure that would be! But I will promise to be on guard father and keep myself from the clutches of any kidnappers. I didn't know there were any here abouts."

Lynton and the Cape Town Ghost

Her father, deeply serious, said, "You have no idea the length to which people will go to accumulate money." He then looked directly at Lynton and continued, "Am I right, Ms. Viñas?"

Lynton, never one to pass up an opportunity to philosophize about the evils of capitalistic society, where greed was promoted as an enviable trait, said, "Unfortunately, yes, you are right. In today's society, the evil of capitalism is prevalent all over the world. The time will come when the poor will rise up with a new spirit of righteous indignation in the land. The days of grab and greed will be tossed, along with the money-grubbing rich, into the dust-bin of history, where they will rot in eternity among the festering bile of evil that has been allowed to reward those at the top with the spoils of their hereditarily ill-gotten gains that have for generation after generation allowed them to benefit off the hard labour of the workers they so willingly exploit. This will usher in a time when no one will want to fill their bellies while others ache for nourishment, a time when no one will want to sleep in a warm bed when others shiver in the cold, a time when injustice against one is considered an injustice against all. Oh, how I long for that time, Mr. Shriver. I dream of that world."

Somewhat taken aback by her discourse on the economics of the modern world and its evil, Shriver was at a loss for words. He was obviously impressed by this woman, who was a keen observer of all that lay before her.

Lynton and the Cape Town Ghost

Lynton excused herself and was walked to the door by Alice, who grasped her hand as Lynton turned to leave and said, "Thank you so much."

Smiling, Lynton did not say anything as she headed down the cobbles. Then she turned to look back over her left shoulder at a forlorn Alice and mouthed the words, "Don't worry."

Lynton was particularly surprised by two things about James Shriver. First, it was curious that Ann Shriver should have married such a man, and even more amazing that she should have confided her daughter and her fortune to his care.

To Lynton, it had always been apparent that the most commonplace people frequently impressed her with the idea that they are other than what they seem, are leading double lives, or are endeavouring to conceal some irregularity of conduct. She had a faculty for reading the natures and characteristics of strangers by studying their eyes, their facial expressions and their oddities of demeanour. Still, she was not sure how to read James Shriver. She wondered if his gruff demeanour was not the real him. Was he, underneath, a kind sort who actually cared for his daughter? If he were not, why would Ann Shriver have trusted so fully a man who displayed such low character? His own child appeared to dislike and possibly even to despise him.

Was he as bad an artist as he appeared? The one painting Lynton saw by him many years before in London was certainly good. She was not an art critic, but that landscape had enough appeal to

Lynton and the Cape Town Ghost

Lynton that she had remembered it after so many years. Perhaps his ambition was too lofty for human skill to realize. Yet, he was capable of at least one fine work of art.

She knew artists tended to be peculiar and often temperamental. They also trended toward moroseness and many suffered from depression. They were often enigmas. And why had he chosen to bring Alice back to Cape Town. It was a place he had abandoned long ago. What was the attraction all of a sudden?

James Shriver had considerable wealth at his command, and although he lived in a mansion, it was not ostentatious. In fact, it was run-down and showed an excess of wear and tear that belied all the wealth he had at his disposal. And why did he sit there in that dilapidated mansion neglecting his daughter's education, ignoring the very least of his responsibilities for her welfare? What had led James Shriver to mysteriously sourer on things and render his life hateful, not only to himself, but to his dear daughter? Over and over again Lynton pondered. Still, despite some despondency she had observed, Lynton reflected on what her husband had once told her, "If there were no night, we would not appreciate the day, nor could we see the stars and the vastness of the heavens. We must partake of the bitter with the sweet. There hopefully is a purpose in the adversities we encounter every day." What was the purpose of the adversities in that mansion on the hill, and what of the apparitions?

Chapter 6
None Other Than Nurse Arnold

Lynton, go so gently though the gate in the fall,
There where the vines cling crimson on the wall,
And in the twilight wait for what will host.
The leaves will whisper there of a ghost.
Like flying words, the sound of misery will fall;
But go, and if you listen, it will call.
Go so gently through the gate,
For there the ghost will await.

No, there is not a dawn in overcast skies
To rift the fiery night that's in your eyes;
But there, where deathly glooms are gathering
The dark shadow is slathering.
Dread is on every leaf that flies,

Lynton and the Cape Town Ghost

For a ghost harbours knowledge of lies.
The dawn comes not at this dark place,
Where a shadow forlornly does pace.

Out of a grave it comes to tell you this.
Out of a grave it wants to say something is amiss.
Piercing flames within your brain are aglow.
You yearn for the way that you must go.
Yes, there is yet one way to where it is;
Bitter, but one that faith may never miss.
Out of a grave it comes to tell you this.
To tell you this! To tell you this!

Through the gate you must not tumble or fall.
Crimson leaves are fluttering on the wall.
Go, for the winds are tearing them away.
Think now of the dead words they say.
You can hear the ghostly agony as they fall;
But go, and if you trust, the ghost will call.
There in the mansion it does await.
Go dear Lynton through death's gate.

One day later, Lynton contacted Alice and asked to visit. She did not see the curt and rude artist, who was somewhere about the grounds keeping out of view; but Alice was ready and waiting, her cheeks flushed and her eyes alight, and she slipped off merrily with Lynton for lunch at Stacked Diner on Kloof Street, where Lynton spent many happy hours enjoying delightful dining where Table Mountain could be seen through the sliding glass panels.

Lynton and the Cape Town Ghost

As they waited for their order, Alice asserted in a sharp voice, "Father is rather disagreeable this morning. He repented his decision to let me go with you and almost forbade me. But I rebelled. I have found that when I assert myself I can usually win my way, for my father, I sincerely believe, is a coward at heart."

Lynton had no retort, but it pained her to see a daughter so thoroughly disgusted with her father. However, she also reflected on the fact that Alice's life and environments were unenviable and that she had lacked, since her mother's death, the affection she needed.

As they dined on thick, juicy hamburgers and fries, Lynton, wanting to know more about Alice's father, said, "You have any idea why your father elected to come back to Cape Town? Wasn't he satisfied in London? Did he not, at least, have friends there?"

"I've no idea," was the forlorn reply from a despondent Alice. "Father seems entirely satisfied with things here, for he has no ambition in life beyond eating three simple meals a day, sleeping from nine at night until nine in the morning and occasionally playing at painting. He corresponds with no one and has no friends as far as I know. But to me the monotony of our existence is fast becoming unbearable, and I often wonder if I can stand it until my age of consent. Then I shall be master of my fate and captain of my soul and entitled to handle my own money, and you may rest assured I will be extremely independent."

Lynton and the Cape Town Ghost

When the luncheon was over and the two girls were wandering about Company's Gardens, Lynton asked, "Did your mother never have any contact with your father after he left when you were a toddler?"

"None. She never spoke ill of him, but frankly, she never really spoke of him at all. Even when I would occasionally, in my early years, ask about him, she generally just passed it off and avoided answering my queries. For that reason, I never was able to accumulate any real knowledge about my father."

"And you were surprised when she left you in his care?"

"Of course. It made no sense to me. I don't know him. Surely someone else more responsible could have looked after me. To his credit, my father is not lavish with what he has at his disposal, but I am sure mamma expected I would have every reasonable wish gratified, and be taught every womanly accomplishment; but I'm treated as a mere unwanted dependent. I'm almost destitute of proper clothing. This dress I am wearing now is the best dress I possess, and I've been obliged to educate myself, making a rather poor job of it, I fear."

Lynton fell silent as she reflected on the litany of woe from Alice. "Alice, there is more to this than just mere neglect on the part of your father. There must be something more sinister going on. What I do not know. However, that ghostly apparition that keeps popping up may be less evil than you think. There may be a just cause it is trying to accomplish in some way," she said gravely.

Lynton stopped at the statue of Cecil John Rhodes, a monument she saw as an abomination. How could the post-apartheid government allow such an avowed racist to be aggrandized with a monument that should be tossed into the dust bin of evil history? She saw Nelson Mandela as a saint among men, but simply could not understand how, when he came to power after his release from Robben Island, he could even allow his name to be used in conjunction with Rhodes at a hotel where she had served an internship. How could two such different men have their names combined on the Mandela-Rhodes Place Hotel? Never were two men more diametrically opposite. Rhodes was a racist who fought to keep black South Africans forever relegated to near slave-like status while elevating Anglo-Saxons, whom he thought superior in every way, to positions of authority to keep the native South Africans from realizing true freedom. Still, her priority now was not reflection on the sordid past of the South African nation, but on Alice Shriver, the apparitions and the depth of what she was beginning to consider to possibly be an outright conspiracy against Alice's emotional, psychological and financial welfare.

As Lynton seemed in deep thought, Alice said, "Father and I are wholly uncongenial and we fight on the slightest provocation. This morning our trouble was over money. I wanted a little to take with me, but not a Rand would he give me. He insisted that if I was to be your guest you would pay all the costs of our day."

"Well, the cost is gladly borne by me for such pleasant company," offered Lynton. "But what does he do with all the income from the trust? Is he saving it for you?"

"I think not. I think he saves it for himself. I think he is hoping I shall die before reaching the age of consent. The irony is that if father was good to me, and kind and loving, I would provide for him in some way after I come into the money."

"It is so strange Alice that your mother trusted him so unconditionally. It doesn't make sense, and neither do these apparitions. I doubted you were seeing apparitions. I assumed they were simply manifestations conjured up by a burdened mind overwhelmed with sorrow and turmoil, but I did see that dark shadow in the doorway, and I heard the moans. Now, I am not saying it was a ghost, but if it was, this ghost is more than just a passing apparition. I believe there is a purpose to its manifestations, and that purpose is not fear."

"What do you mean?"

"I am not sure at this point. I am only postulating at present, and I do not want to say until I am sure."

Lynton took a deep breath and said, "Did your mother not have any in-depth discussion about your father when preparing you for his imminent arrival right before her death?"

"Well, I remember her saying that he loved luxury and all the comfort that money can buy, and so she wanted him to have considerable income to spend, because he was my father and because she felt she had ruined his career as an artist by surrounding him with luxuries during their early married life, and afterward had embittered him by depriving him of them. But the man doesn't know what luxury means, Lynton. His tastes, and I do not mean this is a disdainful or hurtful way, are those of a peasant."

"Yet, once your mother loved him and believed in him. There must have been a reason."

"I think she believed in him; I'm quite sure she did."

"Then his nature must have changed. I can imagine that when your mother first knew him he was hard-working and ambitious. He was possibly even talented, too, and that promised future fame. The painting I saw was very old, so he may have done that when he was first with your mother. But marrying a wealthy woman may have made him lose his ambition, success being no longer necessary. After a period of ease and comfort in the company of your mother, he may have lost both the wife and the luxuries he enjoyed. A man with intestinal fortitude would have developed a new ambition, but it seems your father was not able to muster the will. His return to poverty after your mother's desertion may have made him bitter and reckless. Perhaps it dulled his brain, and that is why he was no longer able to do good work. He was utterly crushed, I imagine, and had not the stamina to recover his former confidence. He must have been many years or so in this condition, despairing and disinterested. Then the wheel of fortune turned and he was again in the possession of wealth. He had now the means to live as he pleased. But those years had so changed him that he couldn't respond to the new conditions. Doubtless he was glad, in a way, but he was now content merely to exist. Doesn't that seem a possibility?"

Alice was amazed at the deductive powers of Lynton. It was in keeping with her reputation for deducing the truth from meagre facts by logically putting them together and considering them as a whole. Still, what did this have to do with the apparitions thought Alice?

Lynton understood the quizzical look on Alice's face. "I know you wonder what this has to do with apparitions, but all this follows a pattern, and it may be providing a roadmap that will offer an explanation for the apparitions. Finding truth is not a thoroughfare. It is usually a circuitous route with hills, bumps, curves and potholes. Be patient as I try to put all the various elements together into a whole."

"But Lynton," said an astute Alice, "Father isn't a man to be crushed. He's shrewd enough, in his own way. Once, in London, a woman, my mother's former nurse, Jane Arnold, made him give her money. I have often thought he ran away from London to escape her further demands. And we saw her at a play with Armand Hardy, who was my mother's attorney."

"Maybe it was back wages she demanded?"

"I do not think so. It was a larger sum than that."

"Won't he have to account for all the money he has spent, when you come of age?" inquired Lynton.

"No, mother distinctly made it so there would be no accounting whatsoever. Her will says he is to handle the income as he sees fit, just as if it were his own, so long as he provides properly for his daughter and treats her with fatherly consideration. That's the only reason he keeps me with him, guarding my person but neglecting the other niceties. If he set me adrift, as I'm sure he'd like to do, I could appeal to the court and his income would cease and another guardian be appointed. I believe there is something of that sort in the will, and that is why he is so afraid of losing me. But he gives me no chance to appeal to anyone. I would go to my mother's lawyer, but I have suspicions about him after seeing him with Nurse Arnold."

"How your dear mother would grieve, if she knew her plans for your happiness have failed," exclaimed Lynton.

"My mother ought to have known my father much, much better," Alice declared sullenly. "I feel extremely bad criticizing her judgment, for her memory is absolutely my most precious possession, and I know she loved me devotedly, but there is one thing in her history I can never understand."

"And that is what," asked Lynton.

Lynton and the Cape Town Ghost

"How could a refined, cultured, well-educated woman like my mother have married my father, an absolute cretin?"

Lynton had a quizzical look on her face. She was silent for a few seconds and said, "I am afraid we shall spend much time pondering that question, as it is the strangest part of the story; and, of course, we can only guess the reason, for the only one who could have explained it properly was your dear mother. However, always remember that love makes strange bedfellows."

They walked over to a nearby bench and took a seat. Lynton, ever sympathetic to poor Alice's plight, placed her hand lightly upon her lap and looked deeply into her eyes with conviction. "Alice I try to never dislike someone based upon first impressions. I do not want to prejudge your father without knowing him better. I do, however, believe he is aware of these apparitions, or at least senses them in some manner. When he came down the stairs as we moved toward the moans and the shadow, I could see a quizzical look upon his face. I believe he at least heard those moans."

"Why will he not admit then to having knowledge of the apparitions?"

"In justice to your father we will, at present, not assume the worst. I must give him credit for not masking his ill nature before me, a stranger. Doubtless your mother understood the man better than we are able to and many years ago, in his youth, talent and ambition were perhaps present. His disagreeable characteristics were probably not so marked then, which may explain why your mother remembers him as he was, not as what he has become."

Lynton took her hand from Alice's lap, leaned back on the bench and continued. "I can understand why you are strongly prejudiced against your father but let us, for the present at least, make due allowance for his bitterness that has manifested itself for whatever reason. I sympathize with you for having to endure, not only the loss of your mother, but at the same time the sudden transfer from the care of a generous and loving mother to that of an ungracious father, a parent you had never before known."

"I am not sure Lynton how much more I can endure. Through it all, my father's disinterest in me has reached epidemic proportions, and he, at least internally, seems to mock my proclamations about seeing what I assume is a ghost."

"Alice, I have, along with you, heard moans and seen a dark shadow, but that is perhaps only proof of two imaginative minds, not a ghost. I have chased what have been called demons, vampires, ghosts, even the devil himself according to people, but I remain a sceptic. I do not disbelieve you, but until I have more concrete proof all I can say is that if we could somehow get your father to admit to experiencing these apparitions also we might be on more solid ground."

They sat in silence for awhile, sweet Lynton contemplating all that she was trying to somehow understand. She was tender-hearted and always assumed the burdens of the weary and downtrodden? She invariably seemed to pick up a trail of sorrow or unhappiness with the eagerness of a bloodhound and once she did, she could not be called off the scent. One small woman cannot regulate the world, but the dynamic dynamo was a tenacious pursuer of truth, justice and plausible explanations, when possible.

She had rarely met so interesting a person as Alice Shriver. The two of them arose and started walking back toward the mansion. All that day the two girls were arm in arm and chatting together, developing their mutual liking.

On the way up Kloof Street, they could not help but stop for desert at Stacked Diner. As they were almost finished, there through the doorway walked Alice's father, approaching their nearby table with a pale white, fear-struck face. His hands were trembling, as he took a seat.

Lynton said, "Good day, Mr. Shriver."

He was as white now as a fresh laundered bleached sheet. He stuttered, "I have seen it."

"Seen what?" asked Lynton.

He did not directly answer her question, only stoically continued to stare off into space as he frightfully said, "Before I had heard something, heard some weird sounds, but today I saw it I tell you. I saw the infernal thing hovering at the top of the stairs."

Alice blurted the words out so loud that those around them turned their way, "You saw the ghost!"

Lynton and the Cape Town Ghost

Still staring straight ahead, as if the two girls were not even there, he muttered, "It was beckoning me I tell you. It wanted me to ascend the stairs. It was trying to lure me."

There are times when the brightness of day is crushed out by the darkness of sombreness. This was one of those times. The remnants of restraint on the part of James Shriver were falling under the dark remnants of thundering fear. There was a stillness that permeated the minds of all three of these people now. It was the stillness of the realization that there was mischief afoot, and this thing, this abomination had been following Alice and her father from place to place. But why?

When the far-gone dead return upon the world, there is generally both rhyme and reason to their manifestations. Had this thing, this shadow of darkness finally decided to make sure that Shriver understood its grave intentions, if they were indeed grave? This thing had, no doubt, been exiled from life, but had refused to go quietly to the grave and rest in the darkness.

Lynton had seen these reactions before, as people were forced to peer into the indefinite unsharpened dawn that offered not the brightness of day but the black of night. This was the beginning of the gloom in the weak-limned hour when ghostly sighs are drained from the souls of the departed and apparitions dance into the minds of those it seeks to instil with fear.

"May I," asked Lynton, "investigate what is going on at your place?"

James Shriver arose, "Of course, why do you think I came here? You are the famous demon hunter aren't you? Come and hunt." He then stormed out of the restaurant.

They looked outside and saw him stop as a woman grabbed him by the arm and he handed her a small envelope. She took it without fanfare, and with a look of obvious pleasure, turned and headed down the street.

"Curious," offered Lynton.

Alice responded, "There is something even more curious."

"What's that?

"That my dear Lynton, that woman who was handed the envelope was none other than Nurse Arnold."

Chapter 7
Come On Sherlock Holmes

Somewhere on an island of the mind
a human-shaped speck casts misery
from the shore of lost hope
into the interminable sea of unrealized dreams.
The lost hope of the mind
contains a cryptic, forlorn note
which bears the agony of one
who long ago lost a lover.
This person lives with unimaginable agony,
and does not know of that which has
befallen his one true love in life.
Pain comes to all,
but to some pain is a constant companion
that forever holds with the grip of constant tears.

Lynton and the Cape Town Ghost

Once on a deserted island of lost hope a man cast a bottle into the sea. It contained nothing but a name, an approximate location and a desperate plea for help so that he might return to cherished ones and know the joy of love once again. He lived out his life on that island, because the person who recovered the bottle tossed it aside, never opening the bottle to read the note. This person had been hurt and cared not for what others were suffering. The person tried to retrieve the bottle many years later, looking desperately for it, but was unable to find it.

Near Cape Town, in Nyanga Township, where the evils of apartheid had been eliminated, but where poverty that accompanied apartheid still festered in the isolation of institutional economic segregation which had continued after black South Africans were released from the bondage of evil that had gripped them under repressive white regime after regime, there was one lone white man living among the predominantly black population. He lived alone in a dilapidated hut on a dirt street and begged for sustenance as he had, long ago, lost the will to lift himself from the misery that had gripped him for years. Despite the rampant crime caused by poverty that forced people to prey upon one another there, he was never targeted, because he was looked upon as a pathetic soul. This was also a man on an island, as he, too, had once sent a bottle in the form of a letter to someone asking forgiveness, but he never received a response. Thus, he sunk into a pit of despair.

Lynton and the Cape Town Ghost

Bottles are cast every day by those in the grips of misery, but in a world where greed and self-aggrandizement are promoted as enviable traits by those who believe all worth comes with monetary value, the bottles are ignored or simply tossed away without concern. This was the way of capitalism, where it is every man for himself. Within this world of tainted values walked Lynton Viñas, a woman who never lost sight of the human equation. She was now on more than just a ghost hunting expedition. She was looking to uncover another, even darker mystery about what was going on with James Shriver. Little did she know, at the time, that the poor soul in Nyanga would eventually play a role in solving this mystery.

The bottle begging for mercy is always bobbing on a sea of turmoil, drifting slowly in and out of view on the crests of passing swells. It glides on mysterious currents with a quiet modicum of hope in a world where most people have little, if any, hope. Life, in a world where economic want is the norm rather than the exception, is like a small ball soaring through space crossing a threshold into a world of darkness that surrounds it. Where is this ball headed? It is in search of companionship with other worlds. The little metal ball floats away as it blinks data back to earth, but the further it goes the fainter the signal, as it is tugged away from that which it was once a part. Thus was this man in Nyanga. He had pleaded only once for understanding, but was denied, and that denial had plunged him into an abyss of darkness.

Lynton and the Cape Town Ghost

In all of South Africa, Cape Town is the crown jewel. It has millions of inhabitants, but in all its aspects it still has a small town charm. The Kloof Street area had been Lynton's home for two years, as she studied for an advanced degree at a local school. Its streets of neat and progressive shops and the business district with broad, tree-lined avenues make it a most pleasant place to call home. Turning off Kloof Street, as the two girls headed toward Alice's house, Lynton reflected on what her husband always told her: "Please darling, try to stay out of trouble. My love for you knows no bounds, but my patience sometimes does. When it comes to trouble, you are like a giant industrial magnet."

She could not help but let out a faint smile, as she knew he said it with love, and when he was away on book tours she somehow seemed to manage to get into trouble. This time was no exception. Then she almost laughed as she thought to herself that the only thing that caused him more worry than her penchant for mystery was her occasional foray into the mall where she might spend too much. Spendthrift that he was, her husband got on-line every couple of days to check the credit card charges. She let out a little giggle, because she knew that she could do whatever she wanted and he would never really get angry. Oh, he might admonish her, but she was a wily girl who knew that the slight tilting of her head, the batting of her dark eyes and the pursing of her lips would immediately dismantle any anger.

Lynton and the Cape Town Ghost

After leaving the park and slightly before the dilapidated mansion on the hill came into clear view, there was a singular projection of loneliness and desolation, where, even in the daylight the vision before the two was darkened with eerie gloom. There was a preponderance of willow trees on the approach to the house that had no rigid trunks with rounded tops and soft outlines, which were continually shifting giving the impression the house before them was somehow alive, but alive with what? Was it alive with the dead? Was this mansion now a conduit for those who journeyed from the dark realms of the hereafter?

As the sky was reddening below afternoon clouds sweeping down from Table Mountain, the girls seemed to move cautiously. Despite being in the middle of a gigantic city, there was a sense of remoteness as the sounds of traffic were muffled to the point of being almost non-existent.

The two entered the mansion, which was empty, save for one servant, a kitchen girl who said she was going out for grocery shopping, bidding the two goodbye. The girls sat in the very room from whence the shadow and moans had emanated. They sat there in silence for awhile, looking about the room as if expecting a visitor from the great beyond. They did not have to wait long. The room seemed to darken, while outside the furious movement of the willows made a whistling sound like one does when walking through a graveyard at night. Above them on the ceiling, a dark shadow began to form. It seemed to just undulate.

Lynton and the Cape Town Ghost

Lynton motioned for Alice to sit quietly. The shadow was darkening, but there was not anger within it, but rather both girls felt a peacefulness all about. A white mist appeared slowly and within that mist there was something forming, something that was not yet discernable. It was something unbidden and unexplained, a curious vision of disquietude, almost of alarm.

The two sat unafraid, but they did have a sense of uneasiness, a sense of awe and wonder. It was not directly felt. Indeed, so vague was the sense of distress that it was impossible to trace it to a source. Was this real or imagined? Had their furtive minds conjured up together this phenomenon before them?

Some essence emanated from the shadow and the now slightly glowing mist that accompanied it. The shadow deepened, growing everywhere without and within darker, floating almost lackadaisically. Within that mist something was becoming clearer now. A black thing was turning over and over inside it. It kept disappearing and seemed to be trying to escape the mist. It was moving upward toward the top of the high ceiling. Suddenly, whatever it was lurched out from the mist. It had the dark eyes of a woman, and they were pleading. They were the saddest eyes either girl had ever seen. They could not make out the face, but the eyes were extremely apparent and the sadness in them cut to the soul of both girls. Not one bit of fear was within either of them, only pity for this poor creature.

Lynton and the Cape Town Ghost

It slowly raised its hands, palms upright in a pleading gesture. It kept gesticulating and making signs of pleading. A low moan vibrated across the room. A melancholy shrill cry sounded overhead, a cry of anguish. Outside, the notorious Cape Town wind was howling in full force. Above the girls was forming within the mist a series of outlines that shifted rapidly. The transparent form floated about. The figure was interlaced with flowing lights, making a great column, and its limbs were melting in and out of view, forming this serpentine line that bent and swayed and twisted spirally with grotesque contortions. They were fluid shapes and all the while the form's face was not discernable.

Lynton could see that poor Alice was becoming extremely agitated, so she motioned downward with both hands to indicate she must remain calm. Lynton could not grasp whether this was real or simply apparitions manufactured by two overactive imaginations. Still, she had been at this so many years that her standard of reality had changed.

Never fearful, the woman proclaimed the dynamic dynamo was possessed with a sense of great awe and wonder at what she was observing. The figure within the mist was floating up, down, left and right. Yet, the dark undulating shadow in a great spiral of grace and strength seemed to have no evil purpose. It appeared to be overwhelmed with sorrow, but with no ill intent. Lynton was sure of that.

Lynton and the Cape Town Ghost

Suddenly, Alice's father entered, and in the blinking of an eye, the dark shadow and the mist were gone. And, once they were gone and the immediate wonder of their great presence had passed, another fear came down upon the two as Alice's father shouted, "What are you two up to in here? What is going on?"

Lynton's eyes locked on Alice's and immediately Alice knew she should speak nothing about what had occurred. She simply said, "We are just relaxing after a day of walking about the Gardens District, father."

Lynton rose and said to James Shriver. "Thanks for allowing me the pleasure of your daughter's company."

As she said that, she glanced over James's shoulder and saw a figure, obviously a woman who had entered with him, clandestinely scurrying from the foyer down the hallway in an attempt not to be seen.

Excusing herself, and telling Alice goodbye while giving a knowing wink, Lynton was beginning to form the nucleus of a profound idea. She thought she knew exactly what this apparition was trying to convey. She could not be sure, but she started out immediately for the coroner's office library on nearby St. Georges Outdoor Mall, where she was about to cull through some books and find out some things that would offer an explanation for what was about to follow in the days ahead. Things that were not self-evident until Lynton lifted the curtain on a dark plot.

Lynton and the Cape Town Ghost

The lonely and seemingly haunted home to which Lynton had cast herself alongside Alice in order to offer the poor girl some solace suddenly flamed up within her mind, as she was leaving the coroner's office, and she felt herself actually trembling at what she was beginning to piece together. She had no proof of her suspicions, but the proof would come later. At the present, she was not as interested in explaining the apparitions as she was in uncovering a sinister plot that had been hatched by some evil doers with nefarious intentions.

Walking through the luxurious Mandela Rhodes Place Suite Hotel, where she had served an internship, she said hello to Xavier, her front office friend, and walked through the revolving door outside. Crossing Wale Street in the Central Business District, she turned onto Queen Victoria Street, heading for her condo at St. Martini Gardens. Uneasiness began to creep over her. As was customary, many men had smiles and a few greeted her with a "hello." Usually responsively congenial, this time she did not return greetings, because she knew something was not right. Someone was following her.

The hairs on her neck pricked up, and she halted by the benches in front of the Superior Court Building. She sat down on the bench that read "Coloured Only," and looked over at the one that said, "Whites Only." The benches were left there as a vivid reminder to all of a sad time in South Africa's history.

She scanned down the street to her left. Then she looked across the street and down the block at St. George's Cathedral at the corner of Wale and Queen Victoria Streets. People were walking briskly, but obviously none of them were following her. Was she just being paranoid?

She rose and began walking toward home, but still she had an uneasy feeling. Hidden from her view was a lone figure that had ducked behind the wall of Company's Gardens Park. Although the person was unable to see her because of the height of the wall, it was possible to glance through the occasional gates that offered entrance to the park.

A cold, grey light filtered down through the clouds overhead, as leaves fluttered about while the wind howled. She stopped in front of the Cape Town Library Branch and stood there watching a ducking figure that seemed like an evil apparition, but it was no apparition.

A bird uttered its cry, and a string of ducks passed with whirring flight overhead in the approaching twilight. The swirling wind was dry and stinging. It was getting more furious now and she held her skirt down to keep it from fluttering up to expose her shapely thighs. She could see across the park, and the same profound yet indefinable emotion of distress seized upon her as she observed the interminable sea of bushes fluttering in the wind. Now she could tell that her follower was definitely a male. Yet, he had a fedora hat pulled over his brow, obscuring his face, making it difficult to get a good look at him.

Lynton and the Cape Town Ghost

All the time her nervousness and malaise increased appreciably. She suddenly found herself overtaken by a sense of vast terror. From the darkness now creeping around the Gardens Restaurant wall, the figure moved swiftly out into the open. Altogether the fear that hovered about her was such an unknown and immense kind of fear, so unlike anything she had ever felt before, that it woke a sense of awe and wonder in her which actually prevented her from immediately realizing that she might be in grave danger. That ominous figure, just as the sense of real danger hit her, suddenly turned and quickly scurried away.

What seemed like an eternity passed, as Lynton went back to her condo, where she lay in contemplative repose wondering whether she should tell her husband about what was going on? She decided against it, because she knew how he worried about her. He often treated her like a child, and she would sometimes say to him, "I am not a child!" Yet, she relished his protective nature. They talked for nearly two hours on Facebook Messenger, and when he asked her if she was staying out of trouble, she felt a tinge of guilt when she lied by saying, "of course."

While Lynton was sleeping, in Nyanga Township, the aforementioned lone white man living in squalor was sitting forlornly in the corner of his small dirt floor hut. He was shivering from the cold and also from recalling days long gone when he looked in the mirror and saw a man with hope.

Lynton and the Cape Town Ghost

He was crying as, having no electricity, he was trying to read by the moonlight peeping in through his lone window an old newspaper he had found. It had blown up from the dump where he foraged for food and clothing. Within that paper, which had been used to wrap a partially gutted fish, was a story from years ago that pierced his mind like a brand searing the flesh of a cow. The tears were for lost opportunity, lost love and lost hope in a life that had simply overwhelmed him. Far too many of us are truly lost souls in a world where there is more heartache than joy. This man put his head into his hands and bawled like a baby.

Outside, people heard his wailing, and they did not dare enter, because it was a familiar occurrence in a place where tears were more frequent than laughter. Tears were prevalent where hope plants no seeds to grow and sprout mighty trees with strong roots that will weather the storm of life. Thus is an economic world where the vast majority of children are born into poverty and will die in poverty, but this man was not crying over his abject poverty. He was crying for something that had been lost and that he assumed could never be recovered.

He remembered the blarney stone,
As he brooded in the moonlight alone.
He cried as he looked at the shifting shadows
That at some moments fell about him thereon.
From a laboured breathing rhythmic swing,
He shaped in his mind an imagining

Lynton and the Cape Town Ghost

To the shade of a woman once well-known,
Who lit his fire and love was sown.

He thought of her from way back,
And remembered things he did lack.
He whimpered: "I am sure you never thought of me,
And how we might get back on track."
And there was no sound but the outside fall of a leaf
As a sad response to his heartfelt grief.
He cried uncontrollably now,
As before his sorrow he did bow.

If only once again to truly see
That would make him all he could be.
He thought once more: "Nay, I'm lost!"
A shape appeared in the far corner to see.
So he rose softly from the floor
And walked into the moonlit shade,
For he had seen a forgotten apparition
From a dream that he would not let fade.

In the grand scheme of things, one second can be an eternity. That night this man who had lost hope somehow felt that his life had truly finally ended because of what he read in a two year old paper that had somehow mysteriously materialized from a garbage dump. He had long ago decided that he wanted death to claim him and end his suffering. In places like Nyanga Township, life is cheap, because the life people are forced to lead is discounted by the privileged as worthless. On this night, this man was embracing death with gusto.

J. Wayne Frye   129

Lynton and the Cape Town Ghost

Leaning against the wall next to the makeshift cloth door held shut by a cloth tie, was something that he had given up on, but still could not completely let go. It was the fruit of his labours for so long, even after he realized he was a talentless aberration in the world which he wanted so desperately to be a success. He walked over and looked down at the many items stacked against that wall, items that he had accumulated out of frustration, because they were not even valuable enough for the people in the poverty stricken Nyanga hell-hole to steal. Nobody wanted him or that which his despicable, useless little bit of talent had produced. He crumbled to the floor and curled up in a foetal position. He could not control his emotional misery, his anguished hopelessness, his deep sense of loss. He could not plead to God for help, because he believed no God existed that would let the economic misery of places like Nyanga trap people in a deep pit of despair from which there simply was no way up. This was the place where dreams went to die. He once had dreams, but those dreams were gone in the blink of an eye. He turned his back on all that he loved, thinking that he was not worthy of the love other men found. His was a life squandered in the hopelessness of his warped and troubled mind. Sometimes, he had a visitor who appreciated his meagre talent, but that visitor only walked out the door with some of those items that lined the walls of the dirt floored hell, where he dwelled in hopelessness.

Lynton and the Cape Town Ghost

Lynton started off the next day with a visit to Alice, because she was convinced there was more than a mere ghost that was the basis of trouble for the little heiress. If she was right, Alice was in more danger from the living than the dead.

When she knocked at the door, Alice answered with a frightful look on her face. She said, "Come Lynton, come quickly."

She followed Alice into the den on the immediate right, where all of the window shades had been closed, making the room as dark as night, save the one ray of fading sunshine that filtered through the open door. Lynton turned, and shut the door behind her and locked it to make sure no one came in to disturb the manifestation that was taking place.

The darkness was more intense now, but the two girls could make out in the far corner a body floating perpendicular to the fireplace mantle. From that body came the low sound of mournful humming which permeated upwards toward the ceiling, growing fainter and fainter until it finally ceased. At that moment, the quiet was near deafening.

Alice and Lynton clutched each other in bewilderment. Before they had time to properly recover from the unexpected shock, they saw the apparent corpse-like apparition turn on its side to face them while still lying perpendicular to the mantle piece. A moment later it had turned completely over, the dead faint face uppermost, staring at the ceiling.

Still, the face could not be made out as it was blurred. Suddenly, the body swung upright and faced them while the feet were still hovering maybe three or four feet off the floor. The apparition glided toward them as they noticed the skin and flesh were indented with small hollows, perfectly formed, and from them flowed a white substance seeming to drip, drip, drip slowly.

The two heard the front door open, and as they turned to look at the locked door behind them, the apparition vanished. A furious pounding on the door, accompanied by shouts from James Shriver demanding to be let in snapped the two out of their trance like state.

"Sorry," said Lynton as she opened the door, "I must have not realized I locked it."

"You realized it. What is going on in here?"

"Nothing, father," replied Alice. "We were just going to sit down for tea and biscuits."

"In the dark?"

"We were about to turn the lights on when you came in the front door," retorted Alice.

"Nonsense!"

Lynton, sensing the situation was about to deteriorate into a shouting match between father and daughter, said, "My fault, sir. As we came in I shut the door and inadvertently locked it. You were pounding at the door before I had a chance to turn the light on."

A stern look upon his face, James Shriver was boiling with anger, as he turned and walked away, uttering, "Nonsense. Nonsense."

Lynton and the Cape Town Ghost

Lynton smiled at Alice and gave her a wink. "You father is worried that we are getting close."

"Close to what?"

Still smiling, Lynton said, "To the real truth about so many things. I am unsure of the depth of conspiracy here, but believe me, there is a conspiracy. My husband writes detective novels, and the more of them I read, the more astute I have become at detecting. Also, I have worked with New York's finest private eye, Chablis Louise Chavez. One thing I have learned from my husband and Chablis is that often the solution to a mystery is right before your eyes, if only you could see through the diversionary smoke screens put up for nefarious purposes. I cannot see it clearly yet, so I shall not reveal to you what I suspect, other than to say that you are, I believe, in no immanent danger, but still be eternally vigilant, because my dear girl there is a plot developed by sinister minds that is slowly but assuredly unravelling.

Lynton left the house and immediately went to the Cape Town Police District Office, where she asked for Detective Danly, who was summoned by a desk sergeant. Danly came out from his office and upon seeing her got a scowl on his face. Strolling over, he said as the scowl never left his face, "Whenever I see you it means trouble. I thought you came here to be a student, and it would save this department a lot of trouble if you would concentrate on that, rather than being a detective."

"Detective Danly, are you a public servant or not."

Shaking his head, Danly replied, "Unfortunately, yes." He turned and headed for his office, as he looked back over his shoulder and chortled, "Come on Sherlock Holmes!"

Chapter 8
Murder on the Fifth Floor

There once was a man named Cash
Who sang of a death in a flash.
He spoke of a white veiled woman,
Who in the dark night was summoned.

A few years ago after a cold dark night,
Someone was killed in the Cape Town light.
There were a few at the scene, and they all agreed
That the woman who suffered had been freed.

Sometimes the truth is hidden by a lie,
As it was when this woman had to die.
She had turned her back on a husband's life,
Realizing too late she had not been a good wife.

Lynton and the Cape Town Ghost

She haunts wearing a long white veil.
She moans and cries with a sullen wail.
Only two know, only two can see
That the ghost wants to be set free.

The truth is forever near,
As the ghost sheds a tear.
The howling wind blows
For those who are truth's foes.

The ghost haunts in a long white veil,
She moans when the night winds wail.
Nobody knows, nobody can see
That the ghost begs to be free.

Danly sat in awe as Lynton wove a tail of murder. Not once did she mention the apparitions that she had experienced for fear he might not take her seriously.

He sighed deeply, reared back in his swivel chair, and said, "You really believe this? You actually think that it is possible that people could be this calculating in planning a nearly flawless murder?"

"I am ready to prove it, but there would need to be an exhumation of Ann Shriver's body and an autopsy performed. I am almost 100% sure she was murdered, and my investigation is also going to resurrect the life of a man who has suffered needlessly for many years, because of a simple misunderstanding. However, I need to find him, and that will be a monumental task."

Lynton and the Cape Town Ghost

Danly stood, took a deep breath and exhaled long and slow. "You the damndest woman I ever seen, Lynton. No wonder your husband calls you the dynamic dynamo."

Smiling, Lynton said, "You gonna get that court order to dig the body up?"

"I can't on this flimsy amount of evidence. It is just supposition on your part. Get me something more solid. I need some link, something concrete that will convince the judge. I am on your side, but I cannot move with what you currently have."

"Then sit tight and keep a lid on this, and if you will back my play I am going to bring down a house of cards that will fall like I am a hurricane roaring ashore."

"Be careful."

"I always am."

More determined than ever, Lynton was now prepared to expose a murder that might provide an answer for the ghostly apparitions, and she also thought she knew why that ghost had followed Alice to London and then back to Cape Town.

She strolled out of the police station and meandered over to a nearby hotel where her Filipino friend Armi worked. Being a front office manager, she had access to other hotels where she might pump some other front office managers for information that was vital to what Lynton had in mind. She needed to know if people had checked into hotels in Cape Town from the Piccadilly area of London several days before Ann Shriver's death.

Lynton and the Cape Town Ghost

Lynton texted Taxify for a cab and the chatty driver kept her from concentrating on the formulation of plans for uncovering a sinister plot that had been years in the making, a plot that was meant to get the hands of some nefarious characters on a fortune. Ever the courteous woman, she gladly listened to the driver tell of his woes in escaping the Congo wars to become a refugee in South Africa and drive for Uber's chief competitor. The world is filled with people who, in desperate situations, must plead to cross borders into safer countries. The cab driver was just one of the millions who had to flee their homelands in order to escape the violence of a world where war was constantly used to keep the poor subjugated to the powerful and rich. Far too many people were unable to escape the wrath of those who saw no value in human life. The corporations, the despots of commerce, the dictators of mayhem and the arrogant power hungry politicians never served the people's interests, but rather, their own. Over hundreds of years, the feudal society had never ended, but only evolved from peasant slavery to the lords of the manor to a society where people were slaves to their corporate masters. This was corporate capitalism at work, where modern wage slavery was the norm as people struggled to make ends meet while those at the top of the economic ladder lived lives of luxurious splendour on the backs of workers. This was the modern world of commerce that talked of economic freedom but embraced economic slavery.

Lynton and the Cape Town Ghost

She was dropped off at an elaborate resort in the Plattekloof area of Cape Town. Her other three Filipino friends had a successful business there. Jasmine, Anabelle and Petchie had all become her good friends, as they met by circumstance through Facebook. She knew them as dependable women who would help her to uncover what was, she assumed, an elaborate plot to take a young girl's fortune and life from her. Time was growing short, because she knew that there was a time frame that made it extremely imperative that Alice die within a short period of time. The plan was as precise, detailed and elaborate as any she had ever seen hatched by criminals who hid behind white shirts, ties and suits to rob and plunder. The real criminals were not those who robbed the corner store to pay for a drug habit or to put food on the table for a starving family. Those people languished in jails run by corporations profiting off human misery. The real criminals were the politicians, the bankers and the corporate C.E.O.'s who cruised about in their yachts, rode through gated communities in their chauffeured limousines and stole more with the stroke of a pen than any robber ever got in a hold-up. If these robber barons were ever caught all they got was a slap on the wrist and a fine. This was called justice in a world where worth was judged by the size of a person's bank account rather than the size of their character.

On this morning, Lynton was hatching the nucleus of a plan to do more than just explore the apparitions that had caused dear Alice so much consternation. She did not want to alarm Alice by telling her that her life was hanging by a thread, because she knew exactly when she was scheduled for death. The plot needed one more element to manifest itself before the final solution to capturing riches would be instituted.

The three girls greeted Lynton with magnanimity as they had all forged a bond of friendship the instant they met a few months ago. They had immediately taken to Lynton's bright and cheerful nature, as she had taken to their kindness toward her and her husband. Being far from home, they all found joy in speaking to one another in their native language and sharing ethnic food.

Five Filipino Women

Under the arch of life, where serenity dwells,
Five girls guard a shrine, where I saw
Beauty enthroned; and I gazed in awe.
I drew in their loveliness with each breath.
Theirs are the eyes which, over and beneath,
The sky above will bend, which can draw
By the spirit for each woman to one law,
The allotted grandeur of heaven bequeathed.

Theirs is that intrinsic beauty, in whose praise
All voices and hands shake still and free.
By flying hair and fluttering hem, the beat
Follows each at the great judgment seat.

Lynton and the Cape Town Ghost

How irretrievably lovely are they,
Who bring sunshine to each day.
But they are not conditioned by strife,
For determined they embrace life.

Their beauty of spirit is a joy forever.
Their loveliness increases; it will never
Pass into nothingness; but still will keep
In the minds of those who gently sleep.
Full of sweet dreams, they are quietly breathing.
Therefore, on every morrow, they are wreathing.
Whisper of the women who sunshine lend:
Lynton, Anabelle, Petchie, Armi and Jasmine.

The three girls knew of Lynton's reputation and investigative prowess, so they were not surprised when she said to them, "I need some help solving a mystery."

"As long as we don't have to deal with ghosts or demons," said a laughing Jasmine, "because we know your reputation."

"No demons, and I will deal with the ghost," replied Lynton. "But believe me, the living are much more dangerous than the dead."

Anabelle laughed. "But you are the dynamic dynamo, so you have absolutely no fear of either."

Petchie interjected, "Yes, and you are always wearing those high heels from hell that were made famous in one of your husband's books. Those are deadly weapons on your feet."

"I have lots of deadly weapons," interjected Lynton.

Lynton and the Cape Town Ghost

Lynton was about to lay out a plan for what she needed from the girls just as her phone rang. It was Armi, who had discovered exactly what Lynton was looking for. A man from Piccadilly had checked into the Taj Hotel on Wale Street just three days before Ann Shriver's death nearly two years ago. He was registered as none other than John Smith. "Wasn't that original," Lynton blurted out loud.

Lynton turned to Anabelle and said, "Do you know anything about art?"

She smiled, looked at the picture on the wall behind Lynton and while pointing at it, said, "I know that is art."

"That will have to do I suppose. Your job is to go to every art gallery in the Cape Town area no matter how out-of-the-way and see if there are paintings that may have been there for years, paintings by obscure artists. My guess is that the paintings will be signed by a man with the initials J and S. They might even have the exact name, James Shriver."

"Done," said Anabelle as she got up and quickly headed out the door.

Lynton turned to Jasmine and Petchie, "Are you two capable of following someone and making sure you are not detected?"

Jasmine, smiling, offered a promise. "We two are like a silent breeze in the garden. We rustle leaves but cannot be seen."

"Good, the man's name is James Shriver, and I need a very detailed account of all his comings and goings. The two of you must conduct surveillance with precision. You can go with me to his house, and you wait for him to come out."

As Lynton and the girls turned off Orange Street and strolled up Kloof Street toward the cul de sac whereupon the dark mansion sat, she was thinking that surely the supreme problem for science to solve is, if it can, whether life, as we know it, can exist without protoplasm, or whether we are but the creatures of an idle day; whether the present life is the entrance to an infinite and unseen world beyond, or the universe is but a dark, soulless interaction of atoms, and life a paltry misery closed by the grave. It now appeared to Lynton, based upon what she and Alice had experienced, that there was definitely something after the grave. She had no religion, so she did not believe that there was an afterlife for the good people where the resurrected frolicked about in heavenly bliss and the evil ones wreathed in misery in a fiery hell where little horned men with pitchforks pricked them for eternity. Yet, all her experiences with the supernatural over the years had planted a seed of scepticism within her in regards to all things seen and unseen.

As they approached the old, dilapidated mansion, it was just getting dark, as only an orange glow filtered through the approaching night as the sun slowly slipped behind the horizon. Deeper beneath the trees lining the street the breeze rustled the leaves and the shadows grew all about them. The pulses of the stars just started to glisten as darkness descended. The flittering fire-flies twinkled. And all about them was silence, save the rustling of the leaves. It was as if the dark mansion sat as a lasting testament to evil that lurked within, but Lynton sensed it was not the evil of a ghost, for the ghost she felt was benign. It was a different kind of evil, the evil of those who would stoop as low as any human could in pursuit of the one thing that made the world a place of eternal darkness, a place where the pursuit of wealth extinguished the light of hope trampling it under the jack-booted evil of greed.

The dark land lay silent and brooding. The last twinkle of a departed sun trailed away completely now, bathing the women in darkness, as even the street lamps only slightly twinkled in the blackness. It was as if the dimming light of love across departed summers was whispering that darkness was growing in a world where evil predominated over good.

Nameless people are lost within the world of darkness that grows about us each and every day, but the breath breathed by women like these still stirred the tree-tops in this darkness that tries to engulf the world with the evil of greed. These women's thoughts and passions were the cause of life; the joys and sorrows that they grasp are but familiar friends, and the end from which we all attempt to flee will not be denied, but having known the glory of women like these makes us realize that the universe may be full of ghosts, not white sheeted grave-yard spectres, but the inextinguishable ghostly elements of individual life, which having once been, can never die, though they blend and change, and change again and again forever.

The darkness they were about to walk into was going to now have a piercing beacon shining into it, a strong, indisputable beacon that said, "We shall not go gently into the night, where darkness wants to embrace us, but rather we will rage against the failing light and fight evil when it rears its ugly head."

Ghostly forms are dancing shadows and lights
That flash on dank morasses. The quick wind
That smites at us by the roadside is the night's
Innumerable dark children. Unconfined
By shroud or coffin, disembodied souls,
Uneasy spirits, steal into the air
From festering graves when the curfew tolls
At the day's death.
And where so ever a murder was done,
In stately palaces or lonesome woods,
Its high inheritance, there, hovering, broods
Something sadly moaning, groaning for solace.

Jasmine and Petchie were shivering, not from the cold, but from fear. Always calm, Lynton said, "You are in no danger. This man has no idea that he is under suspicion by me for complacency in a crime. I must go in now, but wait in stealth here in the dark over by that far tree. I am sure he will come out when I enter, or shortly thereafter. Be vigilant, and make sure you are not seen. I think I know where he will go, but I must be sure."

Knocking on the door, Lynton could see that when Alice opened it that she was thrilled to see her. Alice's eyes glistened with excitement as she rolled them to indicate that Lynton should be careful what she said. Just then, her father came out of the den, and said, "You again," as he walked by her and out the door into the dark, where Petchie and Jasmine adeptly tailed him without discovery.

Grabbing Lynton's hand, Alice excitedly pulled her up the stairs to her bedroom. "I must tell you Lynton that I was in here awhile ago napping when my room had grown cold, and intensely still. I was awakened by the queer feeling we all know, the feeling that there was something in the room that hadn't made itself known physically, but I felt it was here with me. I could sense its presence just as well as I sense yours now. It was so clear, but something kept it from physical manifestation for awhile. Oh, I could feel it wanting to show itself, wanting to make me aware of its presence and to share its anguish; fore I know what you know now. It does not want to perform evil. It wants to share a knowledge of something that must be known by me, maybe by you."

"And you sensed its presence when you drifted off to sleep, as if it was waiting to manifest itself just at the right time?"

"Yes. The room was pitch black, and at first I saw nothing; but gradually a vague glimmer at the foot of the bed turned into two eyes staring back at me: they gave out a sorrowfully dull light of their own. I was frozen with fear. I thought at first that it might well be a projection of my inner consciousness. I had gone deeply enough into the mystery of a morbid pathological state to picture the conditions under which an exploring mind might lay itself open to such a coming admonition; but I couldn't fit it to my consciousness. I shut my eyes and tried to evoke a vision of my mother's eyes, but in a few moments those had mysteriously changed back into the similar eyes at the foot of the bed. It exasperated me more to feel those glaring at me through my shut lids than to see them, and I opened my eyes again and looked straight into that pitiful stare. Yes, pitiful I tell you, so pitiful. I lay in bed, hopelessly wide awake, and tried to keep my eyes shut, knowing that if I opened them I would be overwhelmed with sorrow because of those pleading eyes. Why I asked was she haunting me? Then, with my eyes tightly shut, a dreadfully sorrowful moaning began, and then I seemed to hear the fluttering of large wings, rising above the bed. Those wings made a beastly noise as they seemed to flap, but still I could not open my eyes for fear of what I might see. Oh, but the moaning made tears well up in my eyes, because whatever this was had such pain, such intense sorrow that it pierced clear to my soul. I just cowered there for what seemed like an eternity but, no doubt, was but a very few seconds."

Lynton and the Cape Town Ghost

"Ghosts take many shapes and forms as was described by Thomas Hardy in a book I once read," offered Lynton. "The returning bride, who claims the fidelity of her betrothed; the murdered man who shakes to remorse the murderer's heart; ghosts that lift the sheets at the foot of your bed as the clock chimes the midnight hour; who rise all pale and ghastly from the churchyard and haunt their ancient abodes; who, spoken to, do not reply; and whose cold unearthly touch makes the hair stand stark upon the head; the true old-fashioned, foretelling, flitting, gliding ghost. Who has seen such a one in dreams? Yet, all such ghosts do not manifest themselves to frighten. Some come to warn."

"But why Lynton? Why does it haunt me?"

"I do not think it is haunting you. I believe it is warning you. A ghost usually does not speak. It can moan. It can groan, but it rarely has power of speech. I believe this ghost wants to protect you."

"From what must I be protected?"

"From the evil of those who want your fortune."

Sighing, Alice said, "You mean my father don't you?"

"I am not sure, maybe not. Be patient with me, as I am only beginning to unravel a plot here, and if what I suspect is true, I am afraid it will require bringing in the police to expose a murder."

"My mother?"

"Perhaps, Alice."

Alice lowered her head and Lynton placed her hand on her right shoulder, for she knew that this extraordinary young woman had suffered immeasurably over the past couple of years.

Such a disposition invited confidence in Lynton from Alice, because dear Alice knew Lynton understood her trials and tribulations, and her shock and grief at the dispassion from her cold, aloof, selfish father. There was a bond between the two girls, as if there was a new world forming for them, a world where Alice knew she had a champion in Lynton Viñas.

Alice, with tears forming in her eyes, said, "I am so glad you came into my wretched life Lynton Viñas. I have felt so terribly alone trying to understand my dispassionate father's apparent lack of love, as I know it is difficult to be saddled with the care of an adolescent when he had not seen me since babyhood and had no special interest in me. I have tried to understand as I know his life was wrecked by his separation from my mother. Yet, though he seems distant and uncaring, he did not refuse the obligation so inconsiderately thrust upon him. Although a man of reserved nature, almost a recluse, self absorbed and shrinking from association with others, he accepted the care of me and, without being able to change his disposition to suit the requirements, to his credit seems to have guarded my health and safety."

"Of course, that appears to be the case," replied Lynton as she thought to herself that although possibly true, the man did have complete control of the money.

Still, there had been no indication that he had squandered the money. Lynton could not help but ask, "Did you ever see him waste money?"

She thought long and hard, until she recalled the money he handed Nurse Arnold. She reiterated the strange occurrence to Lynton. Lynton, her curiosity aroused, said, "And was there anyone else with Nurse Arnold at the apartment?"

"No, as I said, we did see her later that same day at a concert with my mother's lawyer, Armand Hardy. I thought it strange. My father said nothing, just stared at them for a brief while."

"It is indeed unusual they would both show up in London at the same time, or maybe not so unusual under certain circumstances."

"What do you mean?"

"Not sure yet, I am just forming several hypotheses at present. There is much still to be uncovered, but things are falling into place slowly but surely. Alice, has your father ever showed you any affection at all?"

"Once, on that day when we went to the concert. It was the only time he came out of his reserved shell with me."

"You have never been able to get beneath his reserve, then. You came to him from a luxurious life, a petted and pampered child, and his simple tastes and unemotional nature repelled you from the first. Is it not so?"

"I'm not sure. I needed sympathy and affection. Had my father been different, had he shown love for me, or even fatherly consideration, I would have responded eagerly. But he ignored me. There has never been any companionship between us other than that one brief time. He has guarded my personal safety, because I am of financial value to him. Nobody could love that horrible man."

As Lynton and Alice explored her father's coldness, Jasmine and Petchie were expertly following James Shriver. Jasmine was on the same side of the street as Shriver, and Petchie was on the opposite side of the street, and they stayed far back, avoiding any suspicion on the part of Shriver.

Shriver walked hurriedly down Adderley Street, the main Central Business District thoroughfare, until he arrived at the Cape Town Central Station, where all the trains from outlying areas came into the city. He stood totally emotionless for awhile just looking toward the constantly arriving trains. As the train from Simon's Town pulled into the station, he perked up. Only a few passengers got off the train, and one, a lady wearing a nurse's uniform came straight toward Shriver. They did not greet one another. The lady simply extended her right hand just as Petchie was snapping a photo of the lady with her I-Phone. Into that extended hand, Shriver placed a thickly stuffed large manila envelope. The woman did not pause in her stride, merely took the envelope and kept walking. Petchie followed the woman, while Jasmine tailed Shriver. They felt like they were in some spy movie, shadowing evil ones bent on death and destruction. Their hearts raced and the blood flowed through their bodies like a river raging through a gorge. Having Lynton for a friend guaranteed excitement!

The lady dressed as a nurse checked into the Mandela Rhodes Suites Hotel. She was the only one who got on the elevator and it stopped on the fifth floor. Petchie took a seat in the lobby near the elevator and waited. She considered calling Lynton with a report but elected to wait for further developments before doing so.

A man carrying a medical bag walked through the lobby, getting on the elevator. It stopped on the fifth floor, and Petchie wondered if, for some reason, he might be going to see the woman.

After about ten minutes of watching people go up and down in the elevator, Petchie noticed the man carrying the doctor's bag come back down, exit the elevator, look in the direction of the front desk area in a very suspicious manner and go over to the far corner of the lobby where the desk phone was. He did not use the desk phone, but took out his cell-phone after placing his bag and a large, obviously well-stuffed manila envelope on the counter beside the bag. Was it the same envelope that Shriver had given the nurse? Was this man really a doctor? If so, perhaps that explained his connection to the nurse. Still, the whole affair seemed sordid and convoluted.

The man left the hotel and Petchie followed him down Adderley Street to the Golden Acre Building where professional offices dominated. She watched him go into a first floor office. She walked over and stood staring at the name for awhile before she took a picture of the door, Dr. Robert Holcomb.

While Petchie was busy following Dr. Robert Holcomb, Jasmine was deftly following James Shriver. For a split second, she thought he might have spotted her, as he suddenly turned around to look behind him when they were walking on Church Street downtown. Just as he stared her way, she very adeptly turned to her right and walked into Click's Pharmacy and stood by the door for a few seconds. She then walked out and spotted Shriver about 500 feet away walking down Queen Victoria Street. As she passed the Mandela-Rhodes Hotel Suites building where Petchie had followed the nurse, she noticed a flurry of activity as the police were swarming into the building. Although curious about what was going on, she did not tarry, but rather hurried down Queen Victoria Street trying to catch up with Shriver who made a right turn into the Huguenot Chambers Court Building. She ran hurriedly to make sure she was able to see where he was going in the building. Fortunately, she got there just as she saw Shriver going into the last office on the left at the far end of the hallway. She strolled down to it and took a picture of the name on the door, Armand Hardy, Solicitor and Barrister.

The world is full of mysteries, some frightening, some wonderful, some of them merely fascinating. The world can be a banal and predictable place, the tracks of daily life so well-beaten and defined that culture is awash with the imbecilic obvious. But on this day, Petchie and Jasmine were beginning to understand the exciting life lived by Lynton Viñas, the dynamic dynamo, where intrigue was the norm, not the exception.

Meanwhile, their friend Anabelle was visiting art shops all over the Cape Town inner city core. After an exhausting search of the galleries and asking the proprietors if they had ever heard of a James Shiver, none offered any knowledge of that name. When asked if they knew of any artist with a name incorporating the initials J.S., they all stated that yes; there was actually a person that signed all his or her paintings J.S. They indicated the paintings were highly prized and commanded a good price, especially for Japanese collectors of landscape paintings. No one knew who the artist really was, but that he had an apparent agent who would show up two or three times a year to peddle maybe a dozen landscapes which were immediately gobbled up by primarily overseas collectors who were paying as much as 100,000 U.S. dollars for them. Apparently, this agent was from London, but no one could ever find out the real name of the painter or where he might live.

The three girls, filled with what they hoped was a wealth of knowledge to assist Lynton in her quest, met Armi at Wimpy's Restaurant and waited for Lynton, who showed up at 6:00 PM.

The five girls sat there filled with excitement, as first Anabelle recounted how she had found that there was an artist who signed all his paintings J.S.

and that they were on the market only a few hours or days before eager collectors gobbled them up for astronomical sums.

Jasmine and Petchie told Lynton about the nurse being handed an envelope by James Shriver, and then Petchie described how she had followed the nurse to the Mandela Rhodes Hotel Suites where a man who was apparently a doctor showed up and came down with what appeared to be the same envelope. She ·showed her a picture on her phone of the name on the doctor's door, and Lynton gasped as she said, "That was Ann Shriver's doctor!"

Jasmine then showed Lynton the picture of the door where Shriver had gone into the lawyer's office, and Lynton again gasped as she said, "Ann Shriver's barrister."

The girls all ordered tea and enthusiastically asked Lynton what it all meant. As she paid the bill, Lynton told the girls to come back to her condo where she would try to give them as much detail as possible on what she knew, but that her deductions were not complete, so there would be only a partial picture at the moment.

They strolled down the St. George's Mall promenade which ended at Wale Street, where the Mandela Rhodes Suites Hotel was located, a place where Lynton had served two of her five internships. The hotel, as it had been earlier when Jasmine walked by, was swarming with police, one of them none other than Detective Danly who was standing at the entrance talking to several other men who were obviously also police. Danly walked over to her and said, "Where there's trouble there is always Lynton Viñas."

Lynton said, "And what is he trouble here Detective Danly?"

"Murder on the fifth floor – a nurse."

Chapter 9
She Was About to Go Into Battle

Frost wrote long ago about a ghost daunted,
A ghost that followed the person haunted.
It had no ill intent in mind as it moaned,
Nor fear to instil as it groaned.
It simply wanted to help undaunted.

The ghost dwelled in a lonely house you know,
And it would simply not let go.
It grandly inhabited the walls,
When darkness slowly falls,
And fear will menacingly flow.

O'er ruined fences the vines shield
The dark lonely Cape Town field.

J. Wayne Frye   157

Lynton and the Cape Town Ghost

The orchard tree has grown one copse
Of wood where the woodpecker chops.
The footpath up to the door is healed.

Alice dwells with an aching heart
In that strange abode there far apart
On that disused and forgotten road
That has no dust-bath now for the toad.
Night comes; the black bats tumble and dart.

The whippoorwill is coming to shout,
Then hush and cluck and flutter about.
You hear him begin far enough away
Full many a time to have his say
Before he arrives to bay fear out.

It is under the small, dim, summer star
No one knows who the evil ones are
That share the unlit place for Alice to see,
As a limb flutters from swaying tree,
And a moan can be heard from afar.

This is a tireless ghost, so slow and sad,
Trying to speak of something so very bad.
But it without voice never sings,
Of the horribly evil things
That destroyed the love Alice once had.

Lynton, looking at the girls, indicated by rolling her eyes that now was not the time to reveal what Petchie had observed in the hotel lobby, as it would muddy the waters and cause delays in what

J. Wayne Frye   158

Lynton and the Cape Town Ghost

Lynton was about to uncover. She looked at Danly with deep perplexed concern as she said, "Detective Danly, what I told you earlier may have some bearing on this case. This nurse worked for a Dr. Robert Holcomb, and she was privy to information that got her killed. You need to get an exhumation order for Ann Shriver and you will uncover a plot that has been hatched by nefarious individuals to steal a young girl's inheritance. Please, I am begging you."

"I told you that without more evidence I simply cannot get an exhumation order. The judge will never allow it. Now, if there is something you know about this murder, tell me every single detail. I already know that she was once employed by Dr. Holcomb, a man with an impeccable reputation who is admired, even revered by all his patients and the public at large."

"I have, in my experience, Detective Danly, found that the line between good and evil is permeable and almost anyone can be induced to cross that line when situational forces come into play. In the case of money, lots of money, evil rears its ugly head in unimaginable ways as people who are normally beyond reproach fall before the altar of greed."

A look of cold, calculating determination on his face, Danly said, "Lynton, since you have been in South Africa, you have caused a parcel of trouble despite solving several mysteries. Still, you tend to skirt the law in the process. I am warning you that if you know anymore than you are revealing I will see that you lose your visa, or even worse, be prosecuted for concealing evidence in a murder."

Lynton replied with equal determination. "I will present you with some irrefutable evidence of another murder connected to this one. Then we'll see about the exhumation order."

She turned, motioned for the girls to follow her and as they walked away Danly stood fuming with anger. Yet, he knew that it was ill-advised to mess with the dynamic dynamo!

Back at Lynton's condo, the girls were in a panicking frenzy, but Lynton said, "Relax, because the police are not going to be helpful, as there are too many high placed people involved in this whole affair. Anyway, they, right now, are more afraid of me than I am of them. You see, Danly knows that I am privy to information that he is, at present, afraid to effectively assess out of fear that he will ruffle the wrong feathers. He knows I am a reliable source for ferreting out information, so he will leave us alone for the time being, until I can present this whole affair to him in a neat, orderly fashion that will allow him to wrap it up and take credit for it."

"But Lynton," said a worried looking Jasmine, "we are not sure of anything yet. You have kept us in the dark about so many things."

"I do not want to reveal the hand I am holding to any of you at this point, because knowledge of what I know might well put you in danger. You all have children, and I am doing it to protect you. I regret having gotten you involved, but there was simply too much to do and too little time to do it without your dependable assistance."

Anabelle blurted out, "We are with you 100%. We will do what we must to solve this. What is out next move?"

Sighing long and slow, Lynton turned to Anabelle and said, "You found that someone was selling consignment paintings from a person signing them J.S. Were they landscapes?"

"I asked specifically, and yes, they were all landscapes."

"And what specific landscapes were they?"

"Well, they had none in their shops, but one woman had a black and white photo she had kept of one from years ago. I took a picture of it," said Anabelle as she held up her phone for all there to see the blurry image.

Lynton and the Cape Town Ghost

"I recognize the background," shouted an excited Armi. "I was there once to visit a friend whom I was helping move. It is Nyanga, a very scary place."

"Yes, Nyanga is a dangerous place filled with crime, disease, poverty and hopelessness," offered Petchie.

Interjected a determined Lynton, "Far too much of the world is allowed to languish in poverty while the few get rich. Is it any wonder that the poor resort to crime in order to survive? They are treated as if poverty itself is a crime, when the real crime is an inequitable distribution of income in a world where there is enough for all if only those at the very top would end their hoarding and avariciousness. However, at this moment our concern is not the ills of social inequality. It is trying to prevent a young woman from being murdered for her money, and part of the solution I believe lies in this place called Nyanga Township. Dangerous or not, I believe within that township is someone who can help solve this whole affair. We must go there to find someone I believe probably lives a life of lonely despair, unaware that he should be a wealthy person, because he has been deceived. He probably lives in obscurity because he has had his spirit crushed. I believe that there is such a perverse deception going on, a deception that has existed for many years, even before the death of Ann Shriver, a deception that has netted a group of people vast sums of money while taking advantage of someone who has probably lived a life of deprivation and misery, while others got rich off the fruits of his labour."

Anabelle blurted out, "Someone with the initials J.S."

"Bingo," replied Lynton.

In the hovel where the only white man in Nyanga Township lived, a young Xhosa woman named Alana stood at the entrance. Within, a lonely man had turned out paintings for many years. He had been cared for by this woman who grew to love him, as she saw his lonely, despairing misery and felt that he had no one who genuinely cared for him. He had survived by selling his paintings to a man from London named Harold Northrop, who would buy them 10 or 12 at a time and pay him a meagre sum that would last him for six months. Then Northrop would return and buy more newly completed paintings. At Northrop's request, he signed them all with the initials J.S., except for one painting that had mistakenly wound up in a London Piccadilly Gallery with the man's real name on it. That had been a mistake, as Northrop did not realize until it was too late that one of the four paintings he sold the gallery had more than the customary J.S. signature. It was that landscape that Lynton had seen in London, a landscape signed by James Shriver.

Some hearts die a slow, agonizing death, shedding each hope like leaves until one day there are none left - no hopes whatsoever. Nothing remained for this man. In this man's face was no infinite capacity for any dreams or illusions. There was a pitiless indifference toward any aspirations or promise. There was an intensity of anguish, despondency, desperation and a myopic view that life offered nothing of value.

In the dirt floored hut was a man who had long ago run out of a desire to do anything but embrace misery and wallow in self-doubt and lost hope. He carried a love for a woman who had turned him out, but Alana loved him despite his affection for another, because her heart was pure and she saw within him a light no one else could see. She believed in him, believed that this poor lost soul carried within a true spark of artistic greatness that was like a shadow of divine perfection. Her love knew no boundaries, as she had eschewed the affections of others to devote herself to a man who loved another.

Alana walked in and said to J.S., "There are five Filipino women in Nyanga asking about a painter. They seem suspicious in nature. Perhaps you should not answer your door today."

J.S. looked at Alana with a heavy heart and said, "Why would anyone be looking for me? I am but a broken down old talentless painter who has no friends, no life and no hope. No one but you Alana and Harold Northrop cares about me."

Alana had always had doubts about Harold Northrop, because she sensed a lack of character in him. He flew in from London two or three times a year and then disappeared. He seemed curt and suspicious. He was dispassionate and appeared to be hiding some dark secret. She had once followed his cab into the Cape Town central business district, where he got out with the paintings in tow and went into the Huguenot Chambers Building and disappeared, perhaps leaving from the rear.

Wayne Frye, Lynton's husband, had always told her that when she walked she reminded him of a song he heard as a teenager. In it was refrain that went, "The way you wiggle when you walk, would make a hound dog talk." Thus, as she and the girls went in search of a painter with the initials J.S., she was causing the usual stir among men. It did not affect her, as she always said that men were simply ninnies when it came to attractive women. They were more interested in the physical than the depth of character. When told she was beautiful, she would always shrug her shoulders and say, "Beauty is transitory and meaningless in the grand scheme of things. Real beauty is like a ripened grape. It can be picked, made into wine, but until it is properly aged it is just nothing but an unfermented grape."

Lynton was a wily, determined woman on a mission, a mission to expose a sinister plot that had been hatched to make some people rich. She was a woman who understood that money was the slave of wise men and the master of fools. These people were willing to go to any lengths to accumulate wealth, and they were willing to take their time to do it. However, with Alice approaching the age of consent, time was now growing short to effectuate a plan that had been hatched long ago to steal her inheritance, and they had stooped to the murder of Nurse Arnold now in order to make sure they were not exposed. These were sinister, calculating, skilled artisans in the fine-tuned art of deception.

Into this unholy mix was also an apparition that kept popping up at inauspicious times, or were they really inauspicious? This apparition had a purpose, and Lynton thought she knew why it had followed Alice from Cape Town to London and then back to Cape Town. This ghost might well be a figment of Alice's imagination, but that did not diminish its impact, its purpose and its means of issuing a cautionary warning of something that was amiss. Lynton was now ready to unleash all her fury to save Alice. She was, as she often did, emulating superman in so many ways. She was about to go into a phone booth, morph into the dynamic dynamo and sprang forth to take on the evil doers.

The girls walked through the trash filled streets their eyes observing the misery and want of those that were victims of a society with no heart. They saw the pain of people ground up in a world ruled by the avaricious selfishness of those at the top of the economic ladder. Their ears heard the sighs and sorrows of those who begged for a modicum of mercy where none was offered. They came to a house where an old woman had directed them, a house where a wreck of a man who desperately wanted to be an artist lived in squalor, pining for some lost love that was gone from a life that had tumbled into an abyss of despair.

Lynton and the Cape Town Ghost

There was no door on which to knock, only a dark and dirty sheet that covered the entrance. Lynton leaned forward and shouted, "Is there anyone home?"

Alana pulled back the piece of cloth and said, "What is it you want?"

Politely, Lynton explained that they were looking for a painter who used the initials J.S., and that she had both good and bad news for him.

J.S., in a low, almost desperate voice, said, "Let the ladies in Alana. And as for bad news, I have had nothing but bad news since the day my wife asked to be rid of me. I cannot imagine anything that could be more horrible than living a life void of my dear wife and child."

"You are James Shriver then?" asked Lynton.

A sigh flowed forth as if he was actually giving thought to a question he should have been able to easily answer. He said, "I used to be."

Lynton and her friends walked into the world that had embraced this man for so long, a world where hope had gone to die. Poverty is hunger. Poverty is lack of shelter. Poverty is being sick and not being able to see a doctor. Poverty is not having access to school and not knowing how to read. Poverty is not having a job, is fear for the future, living one day at a time. Poverty is losing a child to illness brought about by unclean water. Poverty is powerlessness, lack of representation and the total loss of any real freedom; and for most people like this poor man in the hut, added to all those miseries of flesh and spirit is the mental poverty of losing any semblance of hope. This was a man who had not only been defeated by poverty, but by the poverty of mental anguish that wrecks havoc on those who become emotional cripples in a world they cannot comprehend, a world that floods them with self-doubt and a sense of being lost in an endless sea of misery that traps them in the depths despair. Lynton looked at him and fought back tears of empathy, because she saw his pain, felt his sense of hopelessness, and knew she was about to add to his misery. Her voice trembled as she said, "Mr. Shriver, there is no easy way to say this, so I am just going to say it. Your wife, Ann, died two years ago in Cape Town."

Sobbing uncontrollably, he dropped to the floor, as Alana ran to his side, holding him with abiding affection, cradling him like a baby. His sobbing deeply touched the hearts of all the girls.

Looking at him, Lynton realized a light he had carried in his heart for so long, a light that had dimmed but never gone out was now darkened forever. Grief is the price of love. Watching him cry uncontrollably made her realize there is sacredness in tears. They are not marks of weakness, but of power. They speak more eloquently than ten thousand tongues. They are the messengers of grief, of deep contrition and of unspeakable love. She felt that every day from her husband who worshipped and adored her, so she felt the pain of this man in her own heart, because she knew what it was like to be loved unconditionally by someone, and it made her walk over and kneel on the opposite side of Shriver, and like Alana, place her arms around him.

For a good five minutes all Shriver could do was cry, until he finally mustered the composure to say, "I knew it. I found an old paper and read it, but hearing it hurts. And what of my little girl?"

"That is why we are here Mr. Shriver. Your little girl, by the way, is currently fine, but there are those who have hatched a sinister plot to steal her inheritance. And prepare yourself now, as I also believe these people murdered your wife."

He arose and said, "Who are you?"

"I am Lynton Viñas, and these are my friends" she said, as she pointed to each woman as she said their names. "We are here to help you. Here to tell you of a plot that not only led to your wife's murder, but designs to eliminate your daughter and take her inheritance, and also has led to the theft of millions from you, because you are, in fact, a famous artist who has been taken advantage of for many years."

"Famous artist? I have no real talent."

"Oh, but you are so wrong. I saw one of your paintings, the one you did not sign J.S. Today, it is valued at over $100,000 U.S. dollars, and my guess is you have been selling all your paintings to someone who is paying you a pittance."

The shock on his face was palatable. "There is a man named Harold Northrop from England who has bought my paintings for years, paying me no more than 1000 Rand each. He, you mean, has been selling them for vast sums of money?"

Lynton and the Cape Town Ghost

"My guess is, Mr. Shriver, that this man named Harold Northrop has lived in England, lived in squalor similar to how you live here, to give the illusion that he is a man named James Shriver. He paints very poorly under your name and has a reputation for being a failed artist. This was all intentional, so that he could take your place and get control of your wife's fortune after her death. He did this for years as the murder of your wife was carefully planned as was the plot to steal your daughter's inheritance, which is worth far more than the value of any paintings they were peddling. They have been pocketing big money for these paintings by the nom-de-plume, J.S., while they stole your name for nefarious ends that would allow someone to impersonate you to steal all your daughter's inheritance."

"I care not about my fame, my glory, or any money. I care about my daughter. How do we protect her from these unscrupulous cretins?"

Lynton carefully laid out plans that would bring the perpetrators of all this evil to justice. She was determined to not allow the murderers to escape, even if she had to deliver justice herself. Throughout history, it has been the inaction of those who could have acted; the indifference of those who should have known better; the silence of the voice of justice when it mattered most that has made it possible for evil to triumph. Lynton was not going to allow evil to stand triumphant on a mountain of deceit. She was about to go into battle.

Chapter 10
Pleading for Dear Alice's Salvation

From a lost hour a ghost did lean,
But it was no evil spectre seen.
No outward malice did it bring,
Nor from the shadows did it spring.
From hope Shriver had never taken.
From sorrow, he could not awaken.
In his heart there was no joyful tone,
For all he loved, he had loved alone.
Lynton brought news of a black dawn,
And his life was to darkness drawn.
There was a ghost that fed a warning,
As the solution to a mystery was forming.

From every depth of good and ill,

Lynton and the Cape Town Ghost

The mystery held all there so still.
From the torrent, or the fountain,
From the rock cliff of the mountain,
From the clouds that round Shriver rolled,
As the rising sun flashed a tint of gold,
From the lightning piercing the sky,
As it came so quickly flying by,
From the thunder and the storm,
And the cloud that took the form,
These people felt for Shriver so blue,
But, my, oh my, a solution was in view.

The only thing Shriver wanted to do was expose the imposter and free his daughter from the clutches of those who posed a threat to her safety. Lynton understood that and told Shriver that they would go immediately and confront the imposter, and hopefully once Alice was free, go to the police with the new evidence to effectuate an effective investigation. They said goodbye to Lynton's friends as they boarded taxis in Nyanga. Alana pleaded to go with Lynton and James Shriver, and Lynton encouraged her to come, because she saw in Alana a genuine devotion to Shriver, and hoped that somehow he could also see the love she had.

Lynton had been reluctant to cause Alice any more consternation than necessary, but she remembered asking her to review what had transpired in the few months before her mother's death. She was reflecting now back on the conversation they had. Suddenly it became crystal clear how Ann Shriver was killed.

Lynton and the Cape Town Ghost

Lynton frantically pounded on the door of the mansion, and no one answered, not even a servant. Just as they were about to leave, up the cobblestone pathway walked the maid, who looked alarmed as she said, "I went to call the police. Everyone is gone and the locks have all been changed. I was off yesterday, so I contacted the other servants, and they all said they were dismissed yesterday."

None other than Detective Danly arrived and Lynton introduced him to the real James Shriver, as she said, "He is Ann Shiver's legitimate husband. I tell you that Alice Shriver has been kidnapped, spirited away in a plot by these people to escape the law, because they know that they are about to be found out."

"What people," asked Danly?

"First, a man calling himself James Shriver who is actually, if my guess is correct, a gentleman named Harold Northrop, who has been buying paintings from the real James Shriver and stealing millions from him by concealing the real value of the paintings and Dr. Robert Holcomb, along with the barrister, Armand Hardy. The nurse found in Mandela Rhodes Place was also in on it, and her penchant for demanding money to remain silent got her killed by Dr. Holcomb. One of my friends saw Holcomb go up to the fifth floor and leave with an envelope the nurse had, which was incriminating evidence."

Shriver excitedly shouted, "But Alice, my daughter where is she?"

Lynton and the Cape Town Ghost

Alana placed her hand on his arm and said, "Do not fret; it is going to be OK."

Danly went over to the window to the left of the front door, as he said, "Probable cause for a crime means we have a right to enter." He broke the window with his elbow, reached in and unlatched the window, raising it up and crawling in. He went around and unlocked the front door as he called the station asking for a CSI team. He told everyone to stay in the foyer and not move, as he did not want any evidence compromised.

Danly checked throughout the house while the others waited. Coming back in a couple of minutes, he said, "No sign of a struggle in any of the rooms. She may well have gone out of her own volition and will probably come back the same way, when she's ready. We may be making a mountain out of a molehill."

"Why," asked Lynton, "did they change all the door locks?"

"Little Sherlock Holmes," replied Danly, "tell me your opinion."

"Shriver, I mean Northrop, wanted the off-duty maid kept out, because he needed time to escape or to effectuate some part of the plan that was still unfolding, but why he would take Alice is a mystery. He must know, as do the other ones involved, that this whole house of cards is crumbling. Why compound it by kidnapping or harming Alice?" Then she looked to the room to the right of the foyer where the shadow had been seen by her and Alice previously. "Damn!"

Lynton and the Cape Town Ghost

Lynton was not one given to profanity, but this time what was being revealed in her furtive mind had brought words out of that sweet mouth that were not ordinarily uttered. Again she said the word, "Damn! Yes, Northrop knows the jig is up, so he has decided to kidnap Alice, and he, no doubt knows I have found out his real name, found out the original subterfuge practiced on the real James Shriver. He is going to hold Alice for ransom. He is making one last attempt to capitalize financially on a situation that has gotten out of hand. He will try to get a handsome ransom from the estate to free her."

Shriver shouted, "Anything, all of the fortune. The money is of no significance."

Detective Danly, his pride injured, but still stoically recognizing Lynton's perceptiveness, said, "You're a better detective than I am. Girl disappears with fake papa. Real papa, pay up."

"I never realized it at the time, but now so much makes sense. I asked Alice to describe the way her mother was a few months before her death, and I did not think that much if it at the time when she was sharing the information. However, so many things make sense now that I have found the real James Shriver. Ann Shriver was always having some white residue on her lips which was often wiped away by the doctor, the nurse, even Alice herself. There also was a smell similar to garlic. Her complexion was yellowish. There were often lesions on her body and her breathing was laboured and strained."

Danly, a look of intense recognition on his face, blurted out, "The classic symptoms of arsenic poisoning."

Nodding her head affirmatively, Lynton said, "Yes, and the doctor who was helping poison her signed the death certificate, and she was buried unceremoniously right away. The nurse who helped kill her was murdered because she had been blackmailing Hardy, Holcomb and Northrop, as she was impatient about collecting on the inheritance. They finally had enough and the doctor went up to her room and killed her. We have diagnosed the case correctly, and we have to deal with a shrewd, unprincipled and very clever person in the form of Harold Northrop, who is the brains behind this whole affair. He has been planning to steal Alice's fortune for years. It is he who, no doubt, orchestrated the murder of Ann Shriver from his make-shift quarters in London, where, for years he set himself up as the habitually failed artist, James Shriver, building a foundation for his claim to be her father, and even trying to look as much like him as possible. This is all about an elaborate plot years and years in the making."

Danly, impressed with Lynton's perceptiveness said, "With this knowledge that indicates arsenic poisoning, I believe I can get an exhumation order right away."

The CSI team arrived and Danly left with Lynton, Alana and Shriver. Lynton turned to Shriver and said, "You must go back to Nyanga, because that is where the ransom note will probably be delivered.

Now, captivated by Lynton's detecting skills, Danly said, "And what of Dr. Holcomb and Armand Hardy? Should they be arrested now?"

"I think not," replied Lynton. "They are, I am sure, in on the kidnapping, and assume we have not connected them yet. Why not put a tail on them. Keep them under surveillance for awhile before arresting them. They might lead us to Alice or Northrop or both."

"Good suggestion," said Danly.

Suddenly Lynton blurted out, "Wait. Wait a minute. There is one person Alice told me about I have never connected the dots on, one person who was dismissed by the fake James Shriver, but was that a mere act to make Alice think her governess was being discarded. Could she have been another actor on the stage of a sinister play that seems to be slowly unfolding?"

"That is not a bad clue," said Danly. "Her name?"

"Brandy Gorham."

Putting his phone to his ear as they walked away, Danly barked out some orders, indicating a woman named Brandy Gorham should be located, but not arrested. She should be kept under constant surveillance and reports should be made to Danly periodically.

Lynton was always being warned by her husband to avoid trouble. She thought that he was going to be so angry! She could not help it if she was always getting involved in mysteries. She loved them because they required solutions, and for her, solving a mystery was not only interesting but required a definite amount of talent. Since she was a wee thing living in poverty on an isolated farm, she had flooded her mind with the problems at which others shrugged their shoulders. She had turned the problems inside out and canvassed them from every possible viewpoint, questioning this, or that, in search of the most probable solution.

She was empathetic to those in trouble in a world where, frankly, most people had lost the human touch, the empathy for those trampled under the jack-booted tyranny of evil that was devouring hope. After going back to Nyanga with Alana and James Shriver to await the hoped for ransom note, she sat in a corner and arranged in her mind the complete history of Alice, so far as she was informed of it, and made notes in her mind of all facts which seemed to bear on the present problem.

She called Danly and was informed Gorham had not been located. She slept on the dirt floor, wrapped in a warm blanket given her by Shriver, who could not sleep, sitting up all night fretting about the daughter he had not seen in so many years. In the still dark of the morning, they sat despondently, hoping for a ransom note. None came, but something else would. Something else that would groan and moan, pleading for dear Alice's salvation.

Chapter 11
Lynton Viñas on Your Trail

Hereto Shriver never viewed a voiceless ghost;
But now, there is one he is about to see.
Up, down, around, as it is lonely and lost.
It becomes a mist like the morning frost.
Within the barren hut there is no glee,
As sadness is palatable to a high degree.
Where the ghost will next be, there's no knowing:
The grey eyes, and rose-flush coming and going.
Yes, it has so many haunts at last;
Where heard is a moan still and hollow,
As it seems to call out from long ago,
When two lovers were all aglow,
But the stars close their shutters,
And the dawn rises and flutters.

J. Wayne Frye   179

Lynton and the Cape Town Ghost

Dawn in Nyanga, because of its location, seems to linger in incessant darkness as the distant rising of the sun is blotted out by more than just the towering mountains, but by the loneliness, the heartlessness, the misery, the distress, the paucity and melancholy wretchedness of abject poverty. This is the place where human woe and privation is wrapped in a blanket of moral bankruptcy perpetrated by a society that turns its back on the hardships caused by an inadequate and inequitable distribution of the world's tremendous wealth. One of these people who had been lost for so long in this world of barrenness was just beginning to open his eyes after finally, from exhaustion, drifting off into an uncomfortable sleep.

In the dishevelled grimy hut, Lynton and Alana were blinking worried bloodshot eyes at the same time that James Shriver was realizing the three had an uninvited guest. In the far corner, near the cloth door, a light bluish mist was slowly forming as all three of them sat up in awe. Not a word passed between them as within that mist an outline was taking place. A woman with dark pleading eyes was slowly materializing.

For the first time the form of the ghost was completely discernable. It was definitely a woman who reached up and lifted her white veil. When the veil was flipped up on top of her head, James Shriver began to weep uncontrollably as Alana moved to his side and wrapped her left arm around him. Shriver, through tears that were flowing like rain from dark clouds muttered, "Ann."

Lynton and the Cape Town Ghost

A mournful wailing from within the blue mist permeated the darkness. The eyes of the manifestation filled with what appeared to be gigantic tears as the thing pointed a finger toward the ground, and within the dirt of the floor dust swirled about. In the blink of the eye, the apparition dissipated.

John Shriver was crying and shivering, not with fear, but with melancholia for the love he had lost so long ago. Still, at that very moment he realized, as Alana sympathetically tried to console him, that in all this misery there was one constant in his life, one thing that he could always depend on, one person who loved him unconditionally regardless of his dire circumstances. Through those streaming tears, he turned to face Alana and said that which she had longed to hear for so long. "Thank you Alana for loving me. I know that I am a washed up, useless human being, but for what it is worth, I love you, too."

Lynton, her heart filled with joy that in all this misery and turmoil two people had found love, stood and walked over to the place where the apparition had manifested itself. She looked down at the dirt floor, pulling back the cloth door to let in the dim dawn light. There, in the dust were three numbers, *866* and a barely faint word – *Hof.*

Lynton and her husband loved going to the Labia Theatre. (Yes, it is really named that after an Italian princess who built it in 1948.) One block from the Labia was Hof Street. Smiling, Lynton, said, "Sit tight, I'll be back."

Lynton and the Cape Town Ghost

Hof Street meanders up toward the base of Table Mountain in the trendy Kloof Street area. The houses are large, neat, whitewashed Dutch colonials. These houses are completely surrounded by high, very thick block fences with barbed wire at the top that is electrified, so the poor who are always villainized for wanting to survive are discouraged from begging for a crumb from the tables of plenty where the rich dine in their opulent estates. This is the way the rich live with complete indifference to the poor. The old racist apartheid is gone today, but the economic apartheid has never been defeated.

Lynton had no idea what awaited at 866 Hof Street, but as she stood in contemplation by the elaborate gate, where an intercom had to be used in order to be granted entrance, she looked up at the imposing structure that was more palace than home. The windows were so large they reminded her of a giant movie screen. They were obviously triple-glazed and so clear that they appeared to have just been freshly and painstakingly polished to perfection. The birds travelling past, buffeted by the Cape Town winds that whistled through the tall trees, veered off from the property as if reminded they were in some rich, important person's space. The city below Hof Street seemed so far away that it made Lynton feel a chill of isolation from the real world. The ant-like people scurrying about far below and all their problems seemed of no more consequence than the temporary static on the intercom.

A curt, hoarse female voice said over the intercom, "What do you want?"

"I am not sure," replied Lynton.

"Well, then if you are not sure why should you be admitted? Off with you."

"Perhaps I could just ask a question or two, because I am trying to locate a missing girl, and a cryptic clue was given, suggesting there might be knowledge here at this address."

"Missing girl? Who would that be?"

"Her name is Alice Shriver."

"Well, I don't know why you would get this address as a clue, but there was a woman worked here once who used to work for Ann Shriver as a governess."

"Brandy Gorham?"

"Yes."

Now, wanting to speak to her face-to-face in order to more accurately gauge her sincerity, Lynton said, "May we talk person to person, please. This is very important."

Hitting the buzzer made the gate squeakily open and although not told by the voice to do so, Lynton assumed she was to walk up the pathway toward the front of the house. As she started to walk up the entrance steps, from the side, a voice yelled out, "Over here please. Use the service entrance."

"Of course," replied Lynton, as it was obvious that only the exalted were afforded entrance from the front of the house. Her Filipino pedigree meant she had to enter from the side with the riff-raff.

Lynton and the Cape Town Ghost

The woman, seeing Lynton, moderated her antagonistic attitude. "Sorry, I did not mean to be curt with you," said the rather rotund black woman dressed all in white. "I am instructed by the mistress of the house to not waste time with people not on the entry list. She is very strict about who is allowed entry to the grounds."

"Understood," replied Lynton. She extended her hand and said, "I am Lynton Viñas."

Smiling, the lady, as she ushered Lynton into kitchen, said, "I know you. I read about you in the paper. You are that girl who took on those Fascists in the Karoo, and that vampire, and tackled the Stellenbosch terror. You that girl from the Philippines."

"Yes, that is I."

Pointing to the kitchen table, the woman said, "Tea?"

Always aware that engaging in pleasantries made people more open, Lynton said, "Sure. That would be ice."

As the tea perked, Lynton began her subtle interrogation. "So, how long did Brandy Gorham work here?"

"Well, it was not long. She came right after her employer died, and why she came I do not know. She did not seem the domestic type."

She got up, brought over the teapot and poured the tea, then sat back down. "She was a quiet body, never sayin' much to no one. But ladylike, but not very likable I am afraid. In fact, I found her downright unlikable in every way."

Lynton and the Cape Town Ghost

"Can you accurately describe her looks?"

"Well, she ain't tall, but a bit taller than you and she has a nice figure I suppose. Good looking woman she is. Good eyes too, but they seem a bit shifty. She has good manners, but not the kind that make you like her. I take it she's about thirty- five. Very neat an' tidy. Dark brown hair."

"And what made her leave?"

"That's a bit peculiar. She was talking to someone on the phone one day and I heard her say, 'You'll pay up or else.' A few hours later she just up and disappeared. We never heard back from her since then. Didn't even collect her pay."

Lynton rose, thanked her and was escorted to the gate. As the woman closed the gate behind her, she hollered out, "Hope you find her dynamic dynamo."

Lynton, smiling, did not turn around. She just waved her hand in the air and strolled down the street of ostentatious, wealthy arrogance. Being in rich neighbourhoods depressed her. She resented the fact that the few owned the many, because they possessed the means of livelihood for all. The world was governed for the richest, for the corporations, the bankers, the land speculators, and for the exploiters of labour. The majority of mankind were just working people ground down by economic oppression in order for a small number of the arrogant rich to live in luxury. Still, some rich appreciated their largesse and were humbled by their good fortunate. She believed Alice and James would always be humble.

Lynton and the Cape Town Ghost

Where, thought Lynton, do you find someone who apparently does not want to be found? It occurred to her that the ghost's message on the floor offered a way to find Alice through Brandy Gorham. Gorham had been discarded by Harold Northrop while he was impersonating James Shriver. Or had she? Just who was the real Brandy Gorham and why would that apparition leave the cryptic note on the dust of the hovel where James Shriver lived? Slowly, but surely a light went on in the dynamic dynamo's head. Yes, the answer was as easy as getting an American to march with patriotic fervour by waving the flag and shouting Jesus.

Lynton was now connecting a chain of events that were as sinister as any she had ever seen. She recalled how Alice said that there was a scream when the nurse discovered her mother had died just as her father came into the room. It was not the nurse who screamed. Why would a nurse, who was used to death, scream? No, it was Ann Shriver who screamed, who immediately realized that the man who claimed to be James Shriver was an imposter. The shock, combined with the arsenic poisoning, caused a surprised reaction so great that her death was hastened, and she died knowing that her daughter was in peril.

The intricate scheme of Harold Northrop, Armand Hardy and Dr. Holcomb included two women opportunists. These three men had no need for kind souls, they simply wanted compliant accomplices and they got them.

Lynton and the Cape Town Ghost

Human nature in its worst aspects perpetrates selfishness, greed and unscrupulousness. Gorham and Nurse Arnold fit the bill. But why had Gorham spent time at the house on Hof Street? Simple answer, she was told to make things appear normal and avoid suspicion by continuing to work as a domestic when let go by the James Shriver impersonator. However, she could not countenance working for a pittance when she was going to have access to so much money.

Lynton called Alana and asked if there had been a ransom note. There was none. Why?

She then called Detective Danly and found out Dr. Holcomb and Armand Hardy had completely disappeared and that the autopsy had been approved, the body exhumed and the preliminary results showed arsenic poisoning in her system, but that was not what killed her.

Lynton very slyly said, "She was smothered to death."

"How did you know?"

"Because it is common knowledge that there was a scream right after the man posing as James Shriver entered the room. The story was the nurse screamed from shock, but that was just a cover. The scream was from Ann Shriver, who discovered the deception. She could not be allowed to live. The logical solution was to place a pillow over her face and smother her."

With great admiration in his voice, Detective Danly very respectfully said, "Woman, you are something else."

Lynton and the Cape Town Ghost

A bit cockily, Lynton replied, "Of course."

She did not reveal to Danly what she was on to at present, because she wanted to ferret out all the details first. She said goodbye and proceeded to what she assumed would be a rendezvous with destiny.

She had a wealth of information she was deciphering in her head. She was drawing some substantive conclusions as the main facts were becoming lucid and undeniable. Still, she felt that finding Gorham was the key to locating Alice.

Lynton realized that you cannot open a mystery as you do a book. A real life mystery must be delicately and sometimes indelicately pried open. The very fact that Gorham had so carefully concealed her hiding place for years was an assurance that she was a loyal confederate or perhaps nothing more than an opportunist who had somehow put two and two together and managed to cut herself in on what she assumed would be millions down the road. Perhaps she was shrewder and able to show more patience; unlike Nurse Arnold who got herself killed by being unable to wait for the big payoff. Extorting money from murderers is not a very wise course of action, nor was having a woman named Lynton Viñas on your trail.

Chapter 12
He Lit Up Like a Christmas Tree

When by murderers I am dead,
And that you think you are free
From all solicitation from me,
Then shall my ghost come to thee bed,
And the one I protect shall see
That murderers to justice will be fed.

In the shadows I will begin to wink,
And slowly take spectral form,
As you will sense a rising storm.
Your pounding heart will surely sink
As retribution is in the dark born,
And any sleep will from thee shrink.

And then, each murdering wretch,

Lynton and the Cape Town Ghost

Bathed in cold exposure will lie
In far greater pain than am I.
You thought no one would justice fetch,
But sometimes the dead refuse to die.
You murderers will be fate's primal catch.

Alice, grasping the gravity of the situation in which she found herself, realized that she should not have agreed to go with her father when he told her that Lynton had summoned them to the high crime area of Cape Town Flats. How stupid I was she thought as she looked out onto a dirty, debris laden street from the window in the bedroom where she had been put under lock and key. She wondered what her father was up to, and what of the woman's voice she heard in the hallway outside her room? Who was in cahoots with her father to keep her imprisoned?

She knew not her exact location, as it was too dark when she arrived and there were no street signs about. Anyway, she had always been told to avoid Cape Town Flats, as it was filled with knife wielding gangs that were prone to prey upon anyone who was alone and appeared vulnerable. Cities all over the world have areas like the Flats, where the marginalized resort to crime in order to survive in a hostile world where economic privation is the norm rather than the exception. Poverty and crime are the natural result when those with nothing resent any who might have even a little something. The evil of crime is but a stepchild to the evil of economic deprivation.

Lynton and the Cape Town Ghost

As she was staring out the window into the darkness of a world she had always been shielded from, she heard the turn of the lock on the door. Someone was about to enter. To her shock, it was the former governess, Brandy Gorham. Although she despised her, due to the gravity of her situation, she was happy to see a familiar face and could not help but blurt out, "Oh, I am happy to see you."

"I doubt very seriously if you are going to relish my presence little spoiled rich girl."

"How could you be a part of this?" asked a despondent Alice.

"One word – money."

Alice wheeled and in a quick run bounded through the open bedroom door to the stair landing. She looked down below and saw Dr. Holcomb and Armand Hardy at he bottom of the stairs.

"Help!" she cried.

As the two stared up at her, Gorham came out of the room, stood behind Alice and said, "Do you really think they will help you? And screaming will not assist you either. This building hasn't a soul in it but ourselves, and you may yell for help until you are hoarse without being heard. But don't be frightened. I'm not going to hurt you. In fact, I'd like to make your confinement as cheerful as possible. Can't you understand the truth? We are simply holding your person in order to force your real father to anti up a vast sum of money that he will now be privy to."

"What? The man who claims to be my father is not my father?"

"That is right. We have been engaged in a cleaver ruse, but we have been found out by a little busy body named Lynton Viñas. Believe me, when we get the money - someday, somehow, someway we will pay back that little Filipino meddler."

All that Lynton had subtly intonated suddenly was becoming clear to Alice. Her mother, indeed, had been murdered and there was a plot to steal her inheritance, but thanks to Alice bringing Lynton into the situation that plan had been altered. She was kidnapped and trapped in order to rescue her mother's killers from the whole plan being a waste. She was now the goose that sat upon the golden egg, and somehow these nefarious cretins were going to extract some money from someone.

Alice went back into the bedroom, sat down and tried to collect her thoughts. She looked up at a pacing Brandy Gorham and asked, "Do you mind explaining what has happened?"

"No, indeed; I'm glad to explain," replied Gorham, raising her eyelids an instant to flash a glance of approval at her prisoner. "I have been a confederate of your pretend father for years, as he took the name James Shriver and lived in London, while coming to Cape Town and buying your real father's paintings, which, by the way, were very successful in the art world. He is actually, under the initials J.S., a renowned painter."

Lynton and the Cape Town Ghost

You could tell that Gorham was taking a sinister delight in sharing her knowledge of the plot with Alice. "You are mighty precious to all of us, because where we once were waiting a justifiable amount of time to eliminate you, while we drew handsomely from your estate, thanks to your bringing that troublemaking snooper into the whole affair, we were forced to go from killing you so your fake father could get all of your estate to now simply holding you for ransom. Since your estate lawyer is Mr. Armand Hardy, he will go to your real father in a few hours. He, with police acquiescence, will pay 25 million dollars in ransom. We divide up the money and disappear."

"Tell me how you all arranged such an elaborate plot. I know you are going to kill me after you get the ransom, but I would like to know."

Smiling, Gorham said, "Oh, if you are a good girl you may be allowed to live. Still, I can understand your curiosity. Your mother renounced your father when you were scarcely two years old. I met a man named Harold Northrop a few years ago. He, like your mother, actually saw your father had talent, when he inadvertently got hold of one of his paintings and tracked him to Nyanga. It slowly occurred to us that setting up a fake James Shriver and in coordination with your mother's doctor, lawyer and nurse slowly killing your mother with arsenic poisoning would eventually render her estate to your father, because she was so foolishly still in love with him. Unfortunately, Nurse Arnold got greedy and

J. Wayne Frye 193

impatient. It wound up costing her dearly, as you, no doubt, know. Of course, sending you to London was all part of the plan, as we wanted you out of Cape Town so we could more easily effectuate our plan free of official interference. The original plan was for you to have an accident in London, but for some reason Harold Northrop started seeing apparitions, the damn fool, which frightened him, so he came back here, where we planned to do away with you on your next birthday, which would have been a suitable time to avoid any suspicion. Then you met that damnable buttinsky, which threw a real monkey wrench into the whole operation."

Alice stood, turned away and going to the front window, looked through its stained and unwashed panes into the gloomy, debris laden street below. The sight emphasized her isolation from the world. Her imprisonment was becoming unbearable. As she was near tears from building frustration, looking far away in the distance at a vacant lot she saw a lone figure walking briskly through that lot, heading toward the very building in which she was held. This was not an ordinary figure.

A bunch of the boys were whooping it up as
A little determined Filipino girl wanted to pass.
Lynton Viñas walked though the vacant lot;
The kid with the boom-box had it pounding hot.
Someone watched from a window - admiration grew,
For this was a woman who would get her due.

Lynton and the Cape Town Ghost

Out of the darkness Lynton Viñas caused a glare,
As they all looked at her as if she were bare.
They had a snarl on their faces, every dirty louse,
While she strode toward the distant house.
There was none there who had even a clue;
But they were about to also get their due.

There are women who hold hard like a spell;
And you just knew this girl would give 'um hell;
With a dreary stare of a dog whose day is done,
This girl gazed at the menacing men one by one.
They figured who she was, and what she'd do.
This determined little girl was about to brew.

She looked straight ahead in a kind of daze,
Until one of the cretins gave her a menacing gaze.
Another thug looked at her and started to drool.
He didn't realize he was playing the fool.
He walked toward her with an arrogant sway;
But he should have realized this girl didn't play.

The stars were shining and the moon was clear.
Her icy glare was so stern and she had no fear.
She was daring, fearless and cold
Looking them up and down so hard and bold,
While high overhead the sky danced with glee,
Because this was an incredible woman to see.

Lynton Viñas knew how to deal with fiends,
As she called every element at her means;
There was a fire suddenly blazing in her eyes.
This was a woman who was far beyond merely wise.

J. Wayne Frye   195

Lynton and the Cape Town Ghost

A woman dearer than all the world, and true as
Any determined and fearless lass.

The music on the boom box went low,
As the dynamic dynamo attacked the foe.
One thug moved cautiously her way,
But he was about hell to irreverently pay.
She pivoted on her left foot and raised her right
Perpendicular. The high heel was a scary sight.

The heel point stung like a frozen lash;
The man holding his gut, falling with a crash.
She turned her eyes burning a peculiar way,
As her hips began to artfully sway.
Then her lips went into a kind of grin,
As words of wisdom she was about to lend.

She shouted as another moved her way,
"Not a wise move you're making today."
Again her high heels from hell were raised,
As this little girl was totally unfazed.
Delivering another crushing blow,
Her fierceness had a distinct glow.

"Boys, you are making a mistake" said she,
"You thugs must not know me.
But I want to clearly and unequivocally state,
Messing with this girl seals your fate."
Then a stupid one threw a roundhouse right.
Lynton ducked and instantly turned out his light!

One of the thugs screamed loud then,

J. Wayne Frye   196

Lynton and the Cape Town Ghost

Just as Lynton's elbow broke his chin.
He fell to the hard cold ground,
As fear among them was all around.
One of them shouted, "Who's this bitch?"
Lynton replied, "I am the bitch with an itch."

She walked out of the vacant lot
Like a gravedigger who had dug a plot.
She never turned around as she said,
"Remember me boys with dread.
For I am the dynamic dynamo
Who can lay low any foe."

Alice's eyes glowed with admiration for the friend she had made, for the friend who was her champion. Her fear faded as her heart pounded with renewed hope and vigour, but how she wondered did this remarkable woman find her.

The story of how she got to that vacant lot is just one of the many tales of a woman who simply had no fear and no peer when it came to detecting skills or ironed will determination. Cape Town is a place where criminals may securely hide themselves for months, even years without being discovered. The criminals Lynton was after were clever enough to leave few traces behind. As far as clues were concerned they might have evaporated into thin air, except for one slip up that Lynton had discovered.

She had long ago discounted far too many police as corrupt or uninterested in risking life and limb for the safety of those they were supposed to protect. Their actual genuine purpose was being servants to the rich and powerful by keeping the poor and marginalized in line. For that reason, she often detected alone, which she was primarily doing this time, too.

To that end, she tried to ferret out just how to effectively find Brandy Gorham, for she knew that Gorham, no doubt, had Alice with her, and was probably hold up with her three confederates. For all her years in Cape Town, Lynton had primarily used the same cab driver, and he, another Congolese refugee, had a cadre of acquaintances who knew all there was to know about anything and everything. Some were lawful in their actions, and a few were the opposite. Before she wound up crossing that vacant Cape Town Flats lot at night, she had crawled into the back of Donique Burchman's cab and asked one simple question. "If you were a kidnapper, where would you go for an effective hideout?"

"Lynton, you don't want to mess with any kidnappers, because they have made it an art and are as deadly as a cobra in the midday sun."

"I have to mess with them, because someone's life depends on it. I am a big girl and can take care of myself."

As he pulled away from the curb, he said, "Wayne is gonna be mad at me."

"Who are you more afraid of getting angry with you —Wayne or me?"

"I'll take you to meet a guy."

"Good decision," said a smiling Lynton.

Lynton and the Cape Town Ghost

Burchman pulled up very slowly in front of an old dilapidated building in Cape Town Flats on a street that was dark and foreboding. There was a sign out front with most of the lights burned out. It was blinking, and the only words discernable were *afe L mour*. Squinting her eyes to see the missing letters made Lynton realize it said *Café L'Amour*.

Looking back over his shoulder, Burchman said, "Man's name is Spiro. He knows every criminal. You will find him in the booth at the very back. He is always there doing business. It is his office. Maybe I should go in with you."

"I think it better I go in alone. I find men respond better to a woman alone, seems less intimidating."

"I'll wait then."

"No, I will call if I need you to pick me up."

"Lynton, I don't think this is a good idea."

Grinning, she said, "Don't worry about me. I am meaner than a junkyard dog."

Burchman reluctantly pulled away, as he had learned long ago that you simply did not question the methods of this woman. She was someone with an iron will that simply was impenetrable when it came to backing down before adversity.

The front double door with worn brass handles squeaked slightly as she pushed them inward. Dust, cobwebs, dilapidated furniture, broken tables, chairs askew, windows painted over with black, extra dim lamps, peeling wallpaper, gaps in the floorboards, holes in the walls, flickering lights from the once elegant chandeliers with broken strings of crystals, shadowlike people leaning over in whispered conversations and shattered, dirty, cracked old portraits of naked women gave the place the look of long gone elegance that had been replaced by modern hopelessness and despair.

Mildew, rot, the yeasty beer smell, dust flecks floating in the air were the only welcome mat out in this den of lost hope. A phantom hand on Lynton's shoulder and the puff of acrid breath on the back of her neck made her turn around. A feeling of light-headedness and nausea, hair rising on her arms, her body's reaction was to become tense and brace for whatever was about to occur. Through rotted teeth, the tall, imposing man said, "What the hell a dame like you doing in here?"

"Here to see a fellow named Spiro."

The word *Spiro* seemed to send a disarming chill through the man. He pointed to a back booth and said, "That's the man."

"Thank you," said Lynton as she turned and walked toward the back of the café.

Spiro sat at the booth like it was his palace, and he was on a throne. His deep black face was like a piece of worn old oak log that had sat in the sun and rotted for years; his high forehead was knotted fiercely with deep furrows. He had a sinister scowl; his mouth like a knife, his almost smile like the flicker of light across that sharp knife blade. He had a solid black beard, no grey, not even a speck. He was flexing his boney fingers and his scowling eyes were fixated on Lynton's swaying hips moving his way. He seemed to sniff with sharp and private concentration through his long, pointed nose as it crinkled like crisp lettuce. He was probably fifty but looked older. His hair was long, tangled and greasy, hanging down to his shoulders, and he slowly raised his head from staring at Lynton's hips to fixate his eyes like beacons on the face of the gloriously beautiful woman moving so gracefully toward him. He looked scary, imposing and deadly. In her own way, so did Lynton!

Lynton's brown skin was clean and her blissful dark eyes reflected off the dim light above them as she took a seat across from Spiro. Her lips looked like the leaves of a fully bloomed cherry blossom tree; her smile brought the satisfying image of thick, succulent maple syrup being perfectly and slowly poured on freshly made pancakes. Spiro sat mesmerized as he gazed upon her perfect silky form, her skin glistening with natural, not fake sensuality. His eyes were drawn to the brown river that gently caressed its way down her neck, reaching to just below her shoulder blades where delightful mountain peaks separated by a peaceful valley offered a bit of heaven on earth. If God was an artist, Spiro told himself, then this woman was his masterpiece.

With lips that had that freshly licked look, she artfully parted them slowly and deliberately as she said, "I am Lynton Viñas."

Spiro replied, "I have heard of you, and you certainly live up to what I have heard."

"Well, that can be good or bad or both, I suppose."

Spiro, his eyes boring in on hers, said, "It is all good from where I am sitting."

"I will take that as a compliment. Thank you very much."

"You are very welcome, but I have a sneaking suspicion you are not here because of my good looks, but because you seek information that you assume a man of my reputation might be able to help with."

"I am a bewildered woman in search of a young girl whom I believe has been kidnapped by a group of nefarious individuals who might well kill her."

"Don't know why you think I can help."

"Because, according to very knowledgeable people, there is little escapes your scrutiny."

"Compliments will get you a lot with me pretty girl."

"I want to know the whereabouts of a young girl named Alice Shriver. Any tips?"

"I know the Shriver name, but I am afraid I draw a blank in regards to where she might be found. Is she not home with her rich father who has control of her estate?"

"She has disappeared, as has he."

"I have heard that rumour, but again, I have no knowledge of where either of them might be."

"Have you ever heard of a woman named Brandy Gorham?"

"I know the name."

"Any idea where she might be found?"

Spiro looked at a nearby both, raised his right hand and beckoned the occupant over. A man of maybe forty, fairly short, thin as the proverbial rail, with needle marks up and down both arms approached like he was going to worship at the altar of a king. He bowed his head and said, "Yes sir."

Spiro, in rapid fire cadence, said, "Petri, this lady wants some info on Brandy Gorham. I heard the name a few times, but thought you might have more info on her."

Looking over at Lynton, you could tell that he was immediately enamoured with her. Then again, who wasn't? He stuttered out, "I, I, I, yes, yes, I, I knows that woman. She used, used to be, be a governess to some high, high, high toned rich girl. Rich girl's mamma, mamma, mamma died awhile back and the governess, why she fell in love, love, love with a, a, a junkie here in the flats. Junkie died, died, though."

Spiro, with sincerity, said, "This here lady is a friend of mine. She really needs to find this Gorham dame. Can you be of any help?"

"Well, well, well, her junkie boyfriend had, had, had a house that, that, that he inherited and as far as I know, know, know she has lived there, there, there off and on depending, depending, depending on whether she has a job or not, not, not. Since she got fired from that, that, that last job with that, that, that rich girl, girl, girl she has not worked at much. Guess she may still live, live, live there."

"Where's the house," asked Spiro.

"It's, it's, it's actually the only decent house in Khayelitsha. Big 'un it, it, it is. Right across, across, across from Wetlands Park."

"Not far from here," said Spiro to Lynton.

"I need to go tonight," pleaded Lynton, as she looked up at Petri. "Would you escort me?"

"Even with an escort," offered Spiro, "ain't wise to go into that neighbourhood, especially at dark. You certainly won't get no taxi driver to take you there. It is only a kilometre walk. Wait until in the morning. It is safer. You can sleep right here, upstairs. Got a nice little bed you can have, and if you want, I'll even share it with you."

"I cannot wait. Give me directions and I'll walk there now."

Petri said, "You crazy, crazy, crazy lady. Ain't no way anybody, anybody, anybody with any sense walks, walks, walks through Wetlands Park at night."

Looking directly at Petri, her dark, penetrating, sensual eyes pleading, she said, "Please, I need help. Just walk me as far as the park and point out the house. You don't have to walk through the park."

Petri looked dejectedly down at Spiro, who shrugged his shoulders and said, "Walk the lady there. Damn crazy if you asked me, but I done figured out you can't tell this here lady no. It's her funeral."

Lynton and the Cape Town Ghost

Shaking his head frantically from side to side, Petri looked down at Lynton and said, "Let's go, go, go."

Lynton very slowly slid out of the booth and stepped out into the pale light, as her long, dark hair fell in soft layers around her alluring bare shoulders. She had the right physique, the right hair, the right arms, the right legs, the right breasts, the right derriere, the right lips, the right eyes, the right demeanour, the right confident cockiness of someone who knew no fear. She looked down at Spiro and said, "Thanks for your help. If I can ever be of assistance to you, please look me up."

"Lady," said a whimsical Spiro, "You could be a lot of assistance to me, but I got a feeling you ain't interested."

Smiling, Lynton replied, "Got a jealous husband."

They parted with a mutual laugh, as in Spiro's magnified eyes shone a genuine look of concern for her welfare rather than the glee of a gawker. He wanted to reach out and touch her lips, stroke her soft brown skin, caress her with passion in the soft light of the café. Her bare arms were not muscular but toned from hours in the boxing ring, and he noticed her taunt calf muscles flex and her perfectly shaped butt jiggle slightly as she kindly wrapped her left arm around Petri's shoulders in a gesture of thanks and mutual camaraderie. She looked back at Spiro, and for the first time noticed a wheel chair behind the booth seat. Mr. Tough and Rough was an invalid. She smiled at him and gave him a wink. He lit up like a Christmas tree.

Chapter 13
Out of a Nightmare

Ghosts can be guides
When they take sides
Against the evil of the living.

Alice had no guardian angel,
But rather a ghost that would dangle
To warn her of the evil ones.

Into the breech came the dynamic dynamo,
Who could never let evil ones go.
A ghost, a woman and girl – look out!

Petri looked scared, so Lynton smiled and said, "Fear is normal. It keeps you alert."

"Lady, lady, lady they's no way I can go, go, go into that park. I'm sorry, sorry, sorry."

"Don't fret about it. It's OK my dear friend, Petri."

When they got to the park, Petri was trembling almost uncontrollably as he pointed with a shaking hand to a large, old dilapidated huge home about 100 metres across from the park. He said, "Please, please, please don't go. I just can't go, go, go with you."

Lynton, who always said that in reality all humans were drug addicts of one kind or another, felt great sympathy for Petri. Some people were addicted to hard drugs; other people were addicted to sugar, caffeine, food or drink. They were all drugs of one sort or another, which is why she always said that pointing the finger of condemnation was a bit hypocritical when we all have some type of addiction. She got a little smile on her face when she thought of her husband saying he was addicted to her. She reached into her shoulder bag, took out a 200 Rand note and handed it to Petri. He waved his hand indicating, "no," but she said, "Take it for me. It makes me feel good."

He took it and smiled, standing there with tears in his eyes. Like almost everyone she met, he had fallen under her magic spell. He watched the scene in the park in awe of this incredible woman dispatching with ease those who attacked her. As alluded to in a previous chapter, it was utter devastation as Alice looked down at the carnage.

Lynton and the Cape Town Ghost

As Lynton walked away from the panicking havoc of those she had rendered embarrassed and useless, she looked up and saw Alice peering out the window. Like Petri, Alice was in awe of what she had witnessed. Lynton placed her right index finger to her lips to indicate to Alice she should remain calm and not alert anyone to her presence.

Lynton needed help now, and she pulled her cell phone from her purse. There was no signal. She had no time to waste, so she ran toward Petri back past those whom she had dispatched, who were still picking themselves up from the ground and wreathing with pain in the chilly night. She shouted at Petri, "Get back to a phone somewhere and tell the cops, Detective Danly, that Alice Shriver is here. Hurry!"

She turned and ran back through the park, where she was not accosted, because those there had already suffered her wrath and were not eager to tangle with her again. The men she had laid waste to all stood in fascination, watching her as she approached the house in as stealth a manner as possible. She moved to the left of the front door and walked down a small alleyway to the back of the house.

One of those she had brought to his knees looked at his comrades and said, "I pity whoever is in that house if they have pissed that girl off. They are about to taste retribution that will rival a hurricane. Damn, she kicked our asses!"

Another one said, "It was like going up against a buzz saw."

Lynton and the Cape Town Ghost

As Lynton made her way toward the back of the house, in the upstairs bedroom Alice was now surrounded by Hardy, Holcomb, Gorham and Northrop. They handed her a newspaper and told her to hold it up so the date would show. They took a photo. Northrop said, "That will prove she is alive as of today." He turned to Hardy. "Send it along with a ransom note by a courier to Shriver in Nyanga first thing in the morning. We will have him board a private plane and drop the money into coordinates we will only provide when the plane is over the Karoo Escarpment. There will be no time to notify authorities then. You, Armand, will pick up the money and we will all meet at the rendezvous point in Angola. Thanks to that Filipino bitch our plans have gone awry. This may not be what we intended, but we have had two years of being able to steal millions, and now we will get a payoff that will set us up for the rest of our lives."

Alice sat silently as Gorham said, "And what of little missy here?"

Smiling, Northrop said, "She is yours to do with as you please."

There was finality in his words, and Alice knew that Brandy Gorham was capable of murder. It was apparent in the way she looked at Alice, for whom she never had any feelings.

Meanwhile, Lynton had broken a basement window and squeezed her tiny body through the narrow opening. She eased up the basement stairs and listened by the door. No sounds. She went in.

Lynton and the Cape Town Ghost

She made her way through the intense dark to the stairs in the foyer, and at the top landing she saw a dim light filtering from under the door. She surmised that must be where Alice was being held. She contemplated waiting for the police, but this was Khayelitsha, and the police often avoided coming into the area out of fear. The poor were not entitled to the same protections as the rich.

Armand Hardy descended the stairs while Lynton ducked behind a pillar in the hallway, electing not to confront him, as she figured she would fare better with three to one than four to one odds. Anyway, he could be picked up later by the police.

Lynton did not know if any of the culprits had guns, but she knew that Alice possibly only had a few minutes to live, because she assumed that Armand Hardy had left with a ransom note, and since kidnapping was a capital crime, plus the fact two other murders had been committed, there was no reason to assume that they would not also kill Alice.

She elected to burst into the room and surprise them, hopefully catching them off guard; thereby, being able to grab Alice and make an escape in the confusion. She moved up the stairs cautiously until she was right by the door. She reached down and grasped the doorknob. She made a furious turn of the knob and bounded into the room, surveying the positioning of the culprits. Immediately in front of her was Holcomb with a revolver pointed at her. She raised her vaunted right leg and kicked it from his hand and it sailed upward over her head and out the doorway behind her onto the stair-landing. She pivoted; turning her back to Holcomb and ramming the still extended right leg backward, kicking him with her heel in the groin. He crumbled to the floor in agonizing pain. Northrop, who was to the left and slightly behind her, charged at her with his head lowered. She turned, took the heel of her hand and hit him in the forehead, breaking his neck instantly. As Holcomb was crawling toward the door moaning with pain, she stepped over him and moved toward Gorham, who had Alice in a vice-like grip as she backed up toward the window.

Lynton moved within less than a metre of her, looking deep into her eyes with determination as she said to Alice, "Bite the bitch," which Alice did, making Gorham lose her grip. Lynton raised her right leg and the high heels from hell slammed so hard into Gorham's chest she tumbled backwards, breaking the window and fell to the street below.

Alice ran to Lynton and they embraced. Lynton wrapped her arms around her and they turned to leave, but in all the confusion, Lynton had forgotten Holcomb, who had managed to crawl out on the landing where he picked up the gun, pulled himself up and stood at the top of the stairs with the weapon taking deadly aim at the two.

Holcomb, breathing heavily, his eyes red as flames, said, "I am going to enjoy killing you, bitch."

Lynton and the Cape Town Ghost

There are times in everyone's life when they think all is lost, and that the inglorious end has finally arrived and that the final curtain will fall to close the end of the play called *Life*. Lynton's only thought was of Wayne. She had no fear of death, but she feared his misery from her death, because she knew she was the light of his life, as he was hers. The two had found each other across thousands of kilometres in the grand and glorious pursuit of love. They had overcome cultural barriers, minor disagreements and separations to stand at that great altar of affection that is the foundation of what makes humans unique. Lynton shed a tear, not for herself, but for the man whom she knew would be lost without her. She gripped Alice's hand and turned to her. In almost a whisper, she said, "Don't be afraid. I am by your side. We shall enter eternity together as grand friends who refused to bow before evil. Die proud sweet Alice."

Holcomb held the gun with a sinister smile creeping across his face that was still edged with pain from the kick Lynton had delivered, and he did not notice the swirling mist forming to his left and the gradual appearance of an apparition slowly taking form within that mist. It was a woman in white and she reached down and lifted her veil, exposing a lovely, peaceful face, the most peaceful and serene face Lynton or Alice had ever seen. This was a woman at peace and set free from that which had bound her to not haunt, but to guard and protect, to warn Alice of danger.

Alice, recognizing that face, in the soft voice of an angel, said, "Mamma."

Holcomb turned to his left and saw the apparition, saw Ann Shriver there before him. In horror, he dropped the gun, screamed and backed up, tumbling down the stairs to his death.

The apparition looked at Alice, smiled, slowly dissipated and was gone in an instant. Alice and Lynton hugged and then walked down the stairs from the darkness toward the door which led them out of a nightmare.

Lynton and the Cape Town Ghost

Epilogue
You're Welcome in This Neighbourhood

I must be gone to my grave,
Where daffodil and lily wave,
And I please the hapless faun,
That journeys by in the dawn.

As the girls stepped onto the stoop and walked down the stairs, there, standing outside, was Detective Danly with a cadre of officers. By his side were James Shriver and Alana. Alice knew instantly who it was, and she ran forward, threw her arms around him and cried. Alana looked up at Lynton and smiled, because now daughter and real father were united, and they would begin to build new lives together with Alana.

Lynton and the Cape Town Ghost

Lynton said to Danly, as she glanced over at Gorham's body sprawled on the pavement, "There are two more inside that are dead. I am afraid Armand Hardy got away."

Danly pointed toward the park where the thugs she had battled were restraining Armand Hardy. Smiling, he said, "You make some strange friends woman."

Lynton waved at the guys in the park, and one shouted across the street, "You're welcome in this neighbourhood anytime, lady."

The End

Lynton and the Cape Town Ghost

The Real Lynton Viñas (The Dynamic Dynamo)

Every bit as daring and innovative as the fictional character, the real Lynton Viñas, having attended Cambridge School of Law and the International Hotel School, is a marketing and hospitality management professional who is the author of the following books:

Grand Hotels:
Reflections on Timeless Architectural Treasures

Haunted Hotels:
Transitory Dances with the Dead

Astonishingly Remarkable and Unusual Hotels

A *Concise Guide for Operating a Restaurant*

J. Wayne Frye

Lynton and the Cape Town Ghost